Surf Safari Nurse

LP FIC Converse

Converse,Jane
Surf Safari Nurse.

DATE DUE

SEP 2 6 2006		
NOV 02 2006		

Surf Safari Nurse

Jane Converse

Thorndike Press • Chivers Press
Waterville, Maine USA Bath, England

This Large Print edition is published by Thorndike Press, USA and by Chivers Press, England.

Published in 2002 in the U.S. by arrangement with Maureen Moran Agency.

Published in 2002 in the U.K. by arrangement with the author.

U.S. Softcover 0-7862-4626-X (Paperback Series)
U.K. Hardcover 0-7540-7464-1 (Chivers Large Print)
U.K. Softcover 0-7540-7465-X (Camden Large Print)

The text of this Large Print edition is unabridged.
Other aspects of the book may vary from the original edition.

Set in 16 pt. Plantin by Elena Picard.

Printed in the United States on permanent paper.

British Library Cataloguing-in-Publication Data available

Library of Congress Cataloging-in-Publication Data

Converse, Jane.
  Surf safari nurse / Jane Converse.
    p. cm.
  ISBN 0-7862-4626-X (lg. print : sc : alk. paper)
  1. Nurses — Fiction. 2. Surfers — Fiction.
  3. Waikiki (Honolulu, Hawaii) — Fiction. 4. Large type
  books. I. Title.
  PS3553.O544 S87 2002
  813′.54—dc21   2002026646

Surf Safari Nurse

One

A crowd was still milling around the high school auditorium lobby as Laurie Davis's date guided her toward the exit doors.

Most of the now-dispersing audience, as Laurie had noticed earlier, consisted of males, ranging from a small minority of pre-teens through a vast majority of high school and college men. A few, like Ron Tercotte, had brought dates to see the surfing film; most had not.

Near the doorway, behind a long table, a sandy-haired, somewhat plump young man of perhaps nineteen was doing a brisk business selling an assortment of items related to the surfing sport — magazines, glossy photographs, and enormous photographic wall murals. A white T-shirt emblazoned with red letters identified him as a member of LINC ADDISON FILM PRODUCTIONS.

As Laurie and Ron Tercotte passed the table, the tubby salesman interrupted his conversation with a trio of incredibly tow-headed and tousle-haired customers. "Hey, Tercotte! Ron!" He grinned at Laurie's date, then shot a quick sidelong glance at the other boys, as if to record their reactions.

If he had expected to impress them, he was not disappointed. As his greeting was acknowledged with a casual wave, the three blond boys (and Laurie would have sworn that those straw-colored mops had been bleached!) spun around in unison, like puppets manipulated by a single string.

"Ron Tercotte!" one of them muttered. His friends' expressions matched the awe in the boy's voice.

They remained transfixed, staring at the young man at Laurie's side, while the young photo salesman called out, "Have you talked to Linc? He wants to see you, Ron."

"He's got a mob of gremmies around him," Ron said. "I'll catch him at the beach one of these days." His tone implied indifference.

They were talking about the producer of the movie that had just been shown. It had been a thrilling spectacle of monstrous blue-green waves being ridden with grace and deceptive ease on what appeared, by comparison with those formidable walls of water, to be helpless splinters of foam and fiber glass. Laurie had been impressed, not only by the beauty of the scenes unfolding before her, but by the skillful blending of the action with music, and by the smooth, live commentary that had accompanied the film and recordings. From her seat, she had had a poor view of the man behind the microphone, but Linc Addison's arresting personality has made itself known through a voice richer and, if possible, more casual than Ron's.

Ron was steering her toward the exit once more when one of the three boys stepped before them. He was holding a glossy eight-by-ten photograph in his hand and he extended it toward Ron. "Hey, would you autograph this for me?"

Ron's handsome face showed no response at all. Without a word, he flipped a ball-point pen from the inner pocket of his sports jacket and, using a corner of the table for support, scribbled his name across a corner of the picture.

Peering over his shoulder, Laurie caught a glimpse of a half-crouching figure balanced on a surfboard which seemed to be hanging over the edge of a precipice of water; the rider's face was turned from the camera. "That isn't *you,* Ron?"

The trio of boys glanced toward Laurie as though she had uttered something blasphemous. One of them made a smirking sound, indicating the presence of someone with an abysmally low I.Q.

From behind his impromptu counter, the sandy-haired kid said, "Linc got that shot of Ron at Sunset last December." Then, as though he sympathized with Laurie's ignorant state, he added, "That's Sunset *Beach.* In Hawaii."

She nodded dumbly, somewhat bewildered by the idolatrous group that had started to gather around the table, blocking the doorway.

As Ron returned the photograph to its owner, another boy pushed an identical picture at him. "Sign mine for me, Ron?"

The process was repeated several times in the next few minutes, accompanied by a jumble of voices, most of them saying things that were unintelligible to Laurie:

"Did you straighten off on that one, Ron, or did you power underneath?"

"How long a gun'd you use in this Laniakea shot, Ron?"

"You entering the Makaha contest this year, Ron?"

Worshipful admirers! Ron stood in the

center of this enthusiastic hubbub with poise that hinted at a vague boredom, answering the barrage of questions in an unruffled monotone, and behaving in the traditional polite-aloof manner of a movie hero surrounded by his fans.

Finally, with a slow wave of his hand, Ron said, "Okay. Later, huh?"

The group fell back, like courtiers making way for the king's exit, but Laurie noticed that Ron remained the center of their attention as he opened the door for her.

As if to cement the fact that he and Ron Tercotte were more than nodding acquaintances, the photo salesman shouted importantly, "I'll tell Linc you'll see him at the beach. Okay, Ron?"

Ron nodded. "Crazy." Then, perhaps because he knew that mention of the young man's name would raise his stature with the others, he looked back and said, "See you around, Eddy."

Laurie wished that she could have seen Eddy's expression; she suspected he looked ecstatic.

Outside, the cool, damp air came as a refreshing relief after the closeness of the overheated auditorium. During the day, November in San Diego was barely distinguishable from other months, but the nights brought a chill breeze from the ocean. Ron put an arm around Laurie as they hurried toward the school's parking lot.

"You didn't tell me you're a celebrity," Laurie accused.

Ron laughed, making a deprecating sound. "In your league, I'm not."

"Those kids looked at you as though you're some kind of god. I knew you liked to surf, but . . . are you *that* good?"

"I'm one of the top three big-wave riders on the coast." He said it simply, as though he assumed Laurie would have more respect for facts than for false modesty. "Those kids, though . . . they're typical gremmies."

"Typical what's?"

"Gremlins. Beginning surfers. A lot of them spend more time sitting on the beach making surf talk, or tacking pictures up on their bedroom walls, than on a board." They had reached Ron's station wagon, an old wood-paneled relic that had been preserved in pristine condition. Across the moist windshield, someone had used a finger to write "RONNIE RULES!" Ron helped Laurie into the front seat, then stopped to wipe off the laudatory inscription with his handkerchief before settling next to her in the driver's seat.

Maneuvering the old wagon into the sparse nighttime traffic, he muttered, " 'Ronnie Rules!' Isn't that a gas?"

"Somebody must have recognized your car," Laurie said. "Like I said, you're a celebrity. How do they know you? I mean, some of them may have seen you at the beach, but. . . ."

"Oh-h . . . they read the surfing magazines," Ron drawled. "I'm usually in one or the other — you know, pictures and interviews. Then, I've done some commercial work, endorsing a surfboard manufacturer, and posing for surfing thread ads."

"Surfing thread . . . ?"

"Trunks, jackets, sport shirts." Ronnie grinned, flashing a brilliant smile in Laurie's direction. Even in the dim light from the dashboard, the perfect, deeply tanned features made her breath come faster. She could visualize his curling brown hair with its sun-bleached highlights, those penetrating blue eyes and the lean, muscular physique lending masculine glamour to a line of beachwear designed expressly for the surfing crowd.

"Then, I've done pretty well for myself in the contests — Huntington Beach, and especially the big one at Makaha," Ron continued. "The aficionados follow all that jazz. Mostly, though, I guess they know me from the films."

"You weren't in the picture we just saw?" Laurie phrased the question timidly; she hadn't heard Linc Addison mention Ron's name, but then, she hadn't recognized Ron in that still photo, either.

Ron was silent until he had piloted the old "woodie" up a freeway ramp and had blended it with the southbound flow of cars. "No, I've been in all of Linc's other movies, but I got goofed up with finals when he was shooting this one. As one of those kids said, back there, I was conspicuous by my absence." Grudgingly, Ron mentioned that he hadn't "made it to the Islands" in a whole year.

Mention of medical school exams returned Laurie to a conversational sphere in which she felt more at home. "Well, you did yourself proud in your finals last year. Do as well this year, and when you get your M.D. you'll have your pick of hospitals for your internship."

"Sure. Maybe I'll get to go to the Mayo Clinic." Surprisingly, Ron's statement was edged with sarcasm.

"Well, you *could* do a lot worse! *Any* intern would give his eye teeth to go. . . ."

"In *Minnesota,*" Ron said pointedly, "there's a singular absence of ocean waves."

"You're being funny, of course?"

"Uhuh. If you think funerals are hilarious."

"You wouldn't die if you couldn't surf," Laurie scoffed. "A year isn't. . . ."

"So maybe I wouldn't die." Ron paused. "I'd just *want* to, and that's worse."

Incredulous, Laurie pointed out that a career opportunity, especially in medicine, and especially when the doctor-to-be was exceptionally gifted, couldn't possibly be measured on the basis of accessibility of good surfing beaches. "It's a wonderful sport — after tonight, I can see where you'd be enthusiastic about it, but after all, it *is* just a sport."

"Correction," Ron said, and he sounded unbelievably somber. "Correction. Surfing isn't a sport. Not to me, it isn't."

"Then what . . . ?"

"It's a way of life."

"Oh, come off it, Ron! You can't possibly mean . . ."

"And you can't possibly understand." Ron sounded irritable now, but then his tone softened, so that it reflected an almost religious quality. "To know what I'm talking about, you'd have to experience the sensations that go with catching a perfect wave — the exhilaration of a fantastic ride. Look, it's — it's a kind of madness. You're challenging the sea. You're coming at it with a knowledge of the way it behaves in a particular place under particular conditions. Along with the knowledge and the skill, there's love, there's respect, there's fear."

"Fear?"

"*Certainly,* fear! Sometimes it's just fun, but I prefer big-wave surfing. When you've gone over the falls backward on a twenty-foot giant at Sunset, or it closes out suddenly and you're caught in that wild soup, or you get wiped out — lose your balance and your board — and there's the chance of being swept out to sea in that crazy channel because you can't swim against the rip tide that giant surf creates. . . ."

"Ron?"

He stopped his recital. Laurie sensed that he had been talking to himself, anyway, barely aware of her presence.

"Yes?"

"If you're *ever* afraid, why would you . . . ?"

"That's the part I told you you wouldn't

dig. Catch a clean, beautifully formed wave, with the crest blowing around you in an offshore wind. You're flying. You're free. Listen, there's no way to express it in words, so why try? All I know is, there's a sense of achievement that I've never found anywhere else."

Ron had spoken with the impassioned conviction of an evangelist, and Laurie weighed his words carefully before she asked, "Won't you find a greater sense of achievement in an operating room? Four or five years from now, when you begin your practice as a surgeon, when somebody's life hangs in the balance. . . ."

"That's different," Ron said shortly. "It's — oh, come on — don't start giving me that hero-doctor malarkey. Hero-doctors aren't even popular on TV anymore."

"I wasn't talking about phony melodrama," Laurie said. "I was talking about what I see every day of the week. Scrub nurses don't have romantic illusions about surgery, Ron." Laurie hoped she didn't sound too smug when she added, "I think I know something about achievement, though."

"Sure. Just don't try to compare excising some character's gall bladder with a perfect day at Malibu." Ron drove silently after that, his jaw set in a grim line that Laurie had learned to recognize.

When Ron had started dating her, intermittently, two months ago, Laurie had been angered by those sudden thrusts of caustic words. But, just as tonight Ron had told her things about himself that he had never so much as hinted at during their previous evenings together, she herself had discovered other truths about him. One was this terse reaction whenever someone touched a sensitive spot. At the moment, she decided, he didn't want to discuss his future. And when you were hopelessly in love with a man, when you lived in dread that each casual date might be the last, you didn't aggravate him; you changed the subject.

Laurie managed this by asking inconsequential questions about Linc Addison: Did Ron's friend manage to make a living producing surfing films, promoting them through surf clubs and showing them in high school auditoriums? Was the chubby kid in the Linc Addison T-shirt a full-time employee?

Ron relaxed again. "Linc has it made. He earns his bread doing the thing he likes to do best. And let me tell you something — he'd be out on the beaches even if he didn't earn a dime at it. That's *living*."

"That boy — what was his name? Eddy?"

"Oh, he's a class-A gremmie. Linc lets him hang around . . . sends him on errands. He doesn't pay him."

"Doesn't he go to school?"

"Dropout. His folks are loaded, I understand. He's a happy little misfit . . . really out of it."

Later, after hamburgers and coffee at a crowded drive-in, Ron parked the station wagon in front of the stucco building in which Laurie shared an apartment with two other nurses. Without a word, he dropped his right arm around her shoulders.

It was a moment she always waited for — a moment without which the evening would have been a dismal disappointment. Yet, as Ron leaned to kiss her, a familiar resentment stirred inside Laurie. Everything came so easily to Ron; while his classmates struggled to stay in med school, Ron's dentist father supported him in comfortable, if not lavish, style. He breezed through his studies with an absolute minimum of effort, absorbing knowledge like a sponge, and heading for the beach while his fellow medics-to-be read themselves half blind. Tonight, half a dozen times, Laurie had heard Ron's surfing fans refer to his style as "effortless." And Ron's own favorite phrases were, "Don't sweat it," and "Stay cool."

Everything about him was easy and pleasant, with everything he wanted within his reach. He was not conceited — in fact, he seemed barely aware of his extreme physical attractiveness. Nor was there anything arrogant about his possessive act; he casually assumed that Laurie wanted him to kiss her. *Casual* — the word was the whole key to Ron Tercotte's character. Even while she clung to him, returning his kisses with an ardor that frightened her, she could not free herself from the thought that had she rejected him, Ron would have shrugged his shoulders, said something like, "Okay, later for you," and nonchalantly walked out of her life.

It was a relief, then, to have him suggest a beach date for the next Saturday she had off duty.

"Make like you're a surf bunny," he grinned.

"What's a surf bunny?"

"A chick who hangs around surfers but never gets her bikini wet."

Laurie laughed, pleased by the invitation, but warned Ron that she didn't own a bikini. Furthermore, she had some private misgivings about filling out an ordinary bathing suit; three years of all-work-and-no-play training and six months in surgery had contributed little toward a glamorous appearance. She was underweight, and her copper-colored hair and her fingernails were clipped short to facilitate the wearing of surgical caps and the repeated scrubbing of her hands. Lately, even her proudest asset, a pair of heavily fringed green eyes, reflected a tiredness resulting from the vacationless three-and-a-half-year grind.

At the door, while thanking Ron for the evening, she made an effort to sound sprightly and energetic. "I'm looking forward to seeing you surf. Besides, I haven't been to the beach in something like five years."

Ron looked at her as though she had lost her mind somewhere along the way. She added, hastily, "But I love the ocean. I . . ."

"When you really *love* doing something, you *do* it," Ron said.

Later, lying in bed and viewing the evening in retrospect, it seemed to Laurie that Ron had addressed the biting criticism not to her, but to himself. It seemed inconceivable that someone who had chosen to study for a medical career might resent hours taken away from his pleasure. But Ron had implied as much several times tonight.

Most of the medical students and interns Laurie knew lived and breathed medicine. Working for her R.N. degree, she had been possessed by a similar dedication. It was difficult now to respect Ron Tercotte's attitude.

So much about Ron that she vaguely disapproved of! And so little that had any bearing on the fact that she loved him — loved him more than anyone else she had ever known.

Two

"On a day when the surf's up at Wind-ansea," Linc Addison was saying, "you've got to *expect* to be ignored." He looked out beyond the angry shore break, far out to the shifting peaks milling over an outside reef, and then concentrated his gaze on a small group of seated figures, their boards bobbing up and down in a gentle rhythm while they waited for the right moment and the right wave. "Ron's ignoring *me,* too, but with sets like this, I can't say that I blame him."

Laurie brushed the sand from her forearm and readjusted her position on the soft beach. "I haven't been bored," she assured Ron's friend. "Not that I care to qualify as a surf bunny, but I've enjoyed . . ."

Linc gestured toward the riders. "See that peak developing? Ron's got it wired. Watch him."

By some mysterious process that eluded Laurie, Ron had started paddling, rising to his feet at a psychological moment in which his board and the wave seemed to become one. Plunging downward and to his left, Ron raced with the curling wave, his bronzed body outlined sharply against a wall of green water and feathery white spray.

Linc's more professional admiration matched Laurie's. "*Nobody* surfs like that," he muttered. "I know the guy's got to be stoked, but look at that stance. Like he was bored, waiting for a bus!"

"He does everything that way," Laurie commented. "It's all so . . . cool."

Her companion was silent. Ron ended his ride, turning his board around to paddle back through the surf to what Linc had called "the lineup." Then, stretching his slender frame on the sand near Laurie, Linc propped his head up on one elbow and said, "Do I detect a note of bitterness, Miss Davis?"

"Bitterness?" Laurie pretended shock, inwardly disconcerted by the astute observation. "I was paying Ron a compliment."

"I see."

While Linc concentrated on another pair of incoming surfers, Laurie made a surreptitious study of him. Older than Ron by four or five years, he had placid features that matched his suave manner. His eyes, heavy-lidded and gray behind darkly framed glasses, reflected a calm, perceptive intelligence. Like Ron, he was deeply tanned, and the contrast with his sun-streaked yellow hair was rather startling at first sight. He wore what appeared to be an expensive ensemble of beige Bermuda shorts and matching sport shirt, and above his crepe-soled canvas shoes, one of his ankles was tightly bandaged. Except for the recently sprained ankle, Linc had explained earlier, he would be out riding with Ron and the others.

Laurie had forgotten about the line of their conversation, but apparently Linc hadn't. When one of the surfers he had been observing dived from his board in a "wipeout," and the other completed his ride, Linc repeated himself as though there had been no interruption. "I *see*."

"You see what?" Laurie asked.

"That, like me, you're a member of the Tercotte Fan Club. He's too much. Like you say, he's cool, no matter what he's doing."

Laurie sifted the white sand between her fingers, staring and wondering why she should be thinking of Ron's perfectly likeable friend as a disturbing influence. "He was giving you a similar buildup on the way up here this morning."

Linc's face was impassive. "If I could handle a board the way he . . ."

"No, he was talking about your — other talents."

Linc tossed one hand up into the air in a careless gesture. "Ah, yes. Mrs. Addison's gifted child."

"Ron said you're an artist with a camera. Well, actually, I saw that for myself. And you're an expert in the jazz field, and you know all there is to know about synchronizing sound with film. And you write brilliant satirical pieces for one of the surfing magazines. What else? Oh, yes, you're a promotional genius — you know how to drum up crowds and . . ."

Linc closed his eyes for a moment, faking a beatific expression. "Go on. I could listen to you forever!"

". . . and you're terrific at organizing your film safaris so that someone else pays the expenses."

Linc sat upright in an abrupt move. "He said that, huh? I guess I must have talked to him about my next deal. You know, film *costs*. Then, if you want the right guys at the right beaches at the right time, you can't expect them to pay their own expenses and be available when you want them."

26

He went on to explain that he had shot surf film sequences in Peru, on the African coast, in the Canary Islands, in Australia, on Mexico's west coast and at Biarritz, in addition to the best Californian and Hawaiian spots. "To do it right, I decided, you need an angel."

Linc had started to explain his new plan when the surfer who had ditched his board a few moments before came straggling up the beach. He had recovered the board and, dripping wet and disconsolate, was carrying it toward the spot Laurie and Linc occupied. His round face and sandy hair identified him to Laurie immediately, even before Linc called out, "When you going to learn, Eddy? You don't take off in front of Toshi Nomura. You don't take off in front of *anybody!*"

"He *pushed* me," Eddy complained. He dropped his board to the sand, breathing hard from his swim through the surf. "Did you see . . . ?"

"He should have held your head under for a while," Linc said. "You take off in front of Ron on *his* wave someday — he'll wrap your board around your neck. Besides, this isn't a beach for gremmies. It's for class surfers. And the locals don't dig bad manners on their waves, either."

Laurie frowned, darting an annoyed glance at Linc. Eddy looked crestfallen enough without the sadistic lecture. Flabby and surprisingly pale, the boy stood at a respectful distance, avoiding dripping on the others, and shivering like a scolded pup.

Linc shook his head in disgust. "Look, run over and get us something to drink. Milk for me. What about you, Laurie?"

"Something hot would be better. Can you get coffee?"

Eddy Whatever-his-name-was beamed a radiant smile at no one in particular. His disgrace now dismissed, he seemed pathetically eager to please. "You name it, I'll get it. Cream and sugar?"

"Black will be fine."

"Gotcha!" Eddy didn't wait for money or further instructions. He made an awkward swoop to pick up a pair of trousers that lay rumpled in the sand nearby, and hurried across the sand as though he were on a life-or-death mission.

Linc shook his head disparagingly once more, murmuring, "Too much."

"Weren't you kind of rough on him?" Laurie asked.

"He wants to learn, he'd better start following the rules," Linc said, adding, "not

28

that I expect much. Eddy's the original Sad Case."

"I felt so sorry for him, being chewed out that way after . . ."

"Oh, by all means feel sorry for him!" Linc's acid tone was reminiscent of Ron's when something didn't measure up to his standards. "His dad only owns a little bitty chain of drugstores around California. And half the real estate in north San Diego County, plus . . ."

"I *still* feel sorry for him," Laurie insisted. "I remember what Ron called him the other night. A 'happy little misfit.' "

"Ron pegged him right." Linc seemed to assume that enough conversation had been wasted on the kid who apparently served as his all-around flunky. "I was telling you I've lined up a sponsor for my next film safari. By paying expenses, I'll be able to lure some of the top surfers. In fact, we'll be going to the Islands in time for the international contest at Makaha, so they'll jump at the chance to get their way paid, since most of them will be going anyway."

Linc's enthusiasm had carried him away, so that Laurie felt the way she sometimes felt around Ron — as though he were discussing the matter with himself and her presence were superfluous. But Linc did turn toward her, to point up a significant detail. "The kid's coming along, of course." He thumbed in the direction Eddy had taken.

"Eddy's one of the top surfers?" Laurie asked.

Linc released a world-weary sigh. "That'll be the day! No, it seems that my money man is sentimental about his kid. Mr. Barclay's underwriting the safari *with* the provision that Eddy goes along. Eddy *Barclay*," Linc emphasized.

"Barclay Drugstores?"

"Splendidly deduced, Miss Davis." Linc smiled, showing uneven but flashingly white teeth. "This film ought to be a gasser. I've got Toshi Nomura lined up. The Beast, Sven Erikson, Goofyfoot Granz — almost everyone I want is set except Ron, and I should cinch him today."

"You mean for the Makaha contest. I think . . . yes, he'll have three weeks off from school during the Christmas holidays."

"I'm talking about the whole scene," Linc cried. "Hawaii, Australia — the whole three-month bag."

Laurie stared at him open-mouthed for a few seconds. "Ron couldn't do that! He'd have to drop out of school!"

"So?"

"*So?* It's . . . why, it's absurd! In your last year of med school you don't quit to . . . to go playing around on a surfboard. Waste all the time and effort he's already put in this semester?" Laurie made an unbelieving sound, but, unaccountably, she found herself trembling. And, suddenly, seeing the unperturbed look of assurance on Linc Addison's face, she understood her earlier reaction to him. Ron envied the way Linc lived, respecting the fact that he never let his work interfere with his first love. It was Linc's probable influence on Ron that irked her. And because she had no claim on Ron, Laurie made an attempt to laugh off the idea. "It's different with you. You've combined your fun with an income — made a career of it. Ron's not crazy enough to . . ."

"Laurie?" Linc was staring at her with those sleepy-lidded but penetrating gray eyes of his. "Laurie, what's your idea of a good life? Nine to five? Punch a time clock? Scramble on the treadmill all year in exchange for a two-week vacation you're too bushed to enjoy?" He examined Laurie's face closely, but his tone was more philosophical than accusing. "Tell me where you get your values."

She was shaking inside now, not certain that her anger wasn't visible. "I got my 'val-

31

ues' when my folks were critically injured in a freeway crash. I was in my last year of high school, with no idea of what I was going to do with my life after graduation."

"Bad break."

"Bad enough so that neither of them survived. But I watched a team of doctors and nurses try to save them. My mom was lucky. She only lasted four days after the accident. Dad hung on for nearly two months."

Linc had begun to trace zigzag lines into the sand, obviously uncomfortable. "Sorry to hear that."

"It was rough. I would have gone to pieces, except that I found out what I wanted to do. I wanted to be useful to someone beside myself. To . . . *try,* the way that crew at the hospital tried." Laurie stopped long enough to control the incipient tears. She tossed her head back, making a fresh start. "My dad was a wonderful guy, but he'd spent a lifetime chasing rainbows. Schemes, crazy businesses, half-baked inventions. He was on his way to L.A. on some wild goose chase when . . . it happened."

"So you were broke and on your own."

"Uhuh. And I didn't have the kind of scholastic record it takes to rate a scholarship." Scathingly, Laurie pointed out, "You see, I'd had *your* values up until then. Have fun now, tomorrow the *waves* may be blown out."

"Touché, Miss Davis."

"But I got through nurse's training. Try *that* sometime, doing waitress work in your 'spare time.' "

She was beginning to dramatize herself, Laurie decided, sounding like the poor but virtuous heroine in a corny melodrama. Brusquely, she brought her story up to date. "I've got my degree now, and I'm in a profession where I'm needed and respected. End of sad tale." Facetiously, because the atmosphere had become a bit thick, she said, "Them's my values, friend."

Linc shrugged his shoulders. "So you enjoy what you're doing."

"Not always. Working in surgery isn't a picnic. I . . ." Laurie closed her eyes for a moment, shutting out the tiredness. "I can see where lolling around on a beach like this for months at a time might be appealing." Then, suddenly alert again, she blurted out, "But not at the expense of a career."

"You dedicated people," Linc said slowly and thoughtfully, "you work-horse martyrs aren't ever contented unless you see everyone you meet locked up in that square

33

little cage with you."

"If you're talking about Ron, he has a brilliant future as a surgeon. He can surf his head off after hours, once he's established . . ."

"And decrepit?"

"What would he have when he got decrepit and *didn't* have his M.D.?" Laurie got to her feet, brushing sand from her thighs. "It's a silly discussion. Let's give Ron credit for more sense."

Linc was looking out toward the waves once more. "The wind's turning," he said lazily. "Starting to blow onshore now."

"I suppose that has some deep significance, way over my square, dedicated head." Laurie began gathering sunglasses, towel and sandals together.

Linc smiled at her waspish tone. "It means we won't have a beautiful evening glass-off. The form's practically shot now. See what I mean? Ron's coming in." Standing up, stretching his arms over his head, Linc yawned. "One thing Ron knows. You've got to get the good things while they last. 'Cause when they're gone, honey, they're gone for keeps."

Apparently Linc decided that his proposition would be received more favorably if he talked to Ron Tercotte without the presence of a "work-horse martyr." Shortly after Eddy Barclay appeared with the milk and coffee he had been sent for, Linc led the exodus from the beach, roaring off in a foreign sports car chauffeured and apparently owned by the anxious-to-please drugstore heir. He had exchanged only the briefest surf talk with Ron, probably tabling his proposition for a later date.

And though Ron must have known from the other surfers that he was wanted as a member of Linc's safari, he said nothing about it to Laurie. On the contrary, he bolstered her faith in his common sense by describing a new thoracotomy technique he had read about, wondering aloud if Laurie had ever seen the operation performed in that manner.

Their day together ended the way their evenings together had ended in the past. And if Ron's interest in her appeared to remain on the same detached level, at least he promised to call her before the next weekend. Nestled in his arms, imprinting the nearness of him on her consciousness to sustain her during the six empty days ahead, Laurie dismissed the disturbing threat that had been posed on the beach.

Ron wasn't going anywhere. Given enough. . . .

Three

On Friday mornings, Ron Tercotte's Pathology class met at the hospital for lab work. It was because of this circumstance that Laurie had met Ron (introduced to him in the hospital coffee shop by a staff pathologist) and, since then, she had often had her lunch at a cafeteria table reserved for medical students and shared by some of the newer nurses.

On the Friday following their beach date, when Ron failed to make an appearance, she stopped Sid Gruener, one of his classmates, to ask if Ron were ill.

At the cafeteria door, Sid tapped his forehead meaningfully. "Yeah. Sick in the head." An unsmiling scholarly type, he peered at Laurie over his thick glasses and made a wry grimace. "He's konked out."

Laurie drew in a quick breath. "You mean, he's . . ."

"Quit. Dropped out. *Kaput!*"

"Are you *sure?*"

"I talked to him for a few minutes last night." Sid looked ceilingward in an attitude of disbelief. "What makes people like him tick? If I had Tercotte's grades, his *ability,* I'd . . ."

"Did he tell you why?"

The medical student shrugged impatiently, glancing toward a group of friends who had started down the hall toward the elevators. "He said, and I quote, 'I've got something more important to do,' unquote. Rocks in his head. If the army doesn't get him now, the booby hatch *should.*" Sid was on his way to join his group, but tossed a final comment back over his shoulder: "Don't try talking him out of it. All I got for my pains was one of those cool smiles that imply the other guy's a cretin."

In spite of the warning, Laurie made the attempt. After four tries, she finally reached Ron on the phone at his dormitory during her afternoon coffee break.

Ron was apparently in a buoyant, hypercharged mood. "Laurie! Hey, I was going to call *you* tonight. What's up?"

"I just heard some disturbing news, Ron."

"What's the matter?" Ron sounded blithely unaware that his decision might have caused a devastating reaction in someone else.

"I talked to Sid Gruener. He says you've quit school."

"Oh, *that*." Ron's pleased chuckle had overtones of relief. "You sounded like something was wrong."

"Ron, you can't do a stupid thing like this! Please don't throw away . . ."

"Hey, what *is* this? I get a terrific opportunity to . . ."

"You've got your opportunity right where you are. Get your degree. You're only months away from . . ."

"Look, I'm not in the mood for a lecture. You don't even know what it's all about."

"I talked to Linc. I know. Ron, you're mature enough to put first things first. You . . ." Laurie hesitated, hoping to get the embarrassing quaver out of her voice. "You can go to the Islands . . ."

"*Later?*" Ron's incisive tone came over the wires like a spurt of acid. "Listen, I'm all jazzed about this trip. I was looking forward to telling you all about it tomorrow night, but if you think I'm going to sit around listening to a maternal lecture,

38

you've got it all wrong."

"I'm only thinking of your own good."

"Uhuh. Well, what makes you think you know more about what's good for me than I do?"

There was a stifling silence, during which Laurie's heavy breathing filled the cubicle of the phone booth. Her legs had started to tremble under her, and she felt sudden, overwhelming shame. What right *did* she have to tell Ron what to do? He was reminding her that her possessiveness was unwarranted; the blow to her pride was worse than a physical slap. "I'm sorry I mentioned it," she said quietly.

"Groovy. I've already gotten the square message from my folks. So now, if you want to talk about something else, let's set a date for tomorrow night and I'll . . ."

"I don't want to talk about anything else." The receiver shook in Laurie's hands. "I don't think I have anything to say that you'd want to hear."

"Well. It's like that."

She managed to swallow back tears long enough to say, "It's like that."

"Okay. Later. I'll see you around, Laurie."

Undisturbed, unaffected, he was saying good-bye to her as carelessly as he had

39

addressed the "happy little misfit" after the surf movie! Either he had ice water in his veins, or she meant nothing at all to him. Laurie replaced the receiver, the full impact of Ron's words pressing against her lungs like some unbearably heavy object.

"I'll see you around." In Ron's language, that meant that it made no difference to him whether or not he ever saw her again. And in a few weeks he would be gone; even the hope of an accidental meeting at the hospital would be severed. *Never.* She would *never* see Ron again!

For an interminable period, Laurie remained in the airless booth, every muscle in her body paralyzed by the grim realization. Later, she remembered going to the nurses' lounge to dab cold water over tear-swollen eyes. And, only vaguely, she remembered scrubbing for an emergency splenectomy that began at two-fifteen and would keep her in the operating room overtime.

She remembered, too, the tense nervous condition of her hands, and, several times, the curt admonitions of Dr. Bateman and the surgical resident who assisted him:

"I said I wanted a long right angle clamp. Stat!"

"A right angle clamp! What's wrong with you?"

"We haven't got all day, nurse; pack off those small bleeders!"

"Where did you train, anyway? When I want a coagulant, I don't want it next week!"

The chief resident was always irritable, but Dr. Bateman had never shouted at her before. Nor had there ever been any hesitation before in slapping the right instrument into a surgeon's gloved hand. Usually, the orders were anticipated. This time there had been errors, needless delays in a procedure that demanded split-second timing.

Laurie released an exhausted sigh as the patient was wheeled to the recovery room. Pulling off his gloves, the elder doctor murmured, "That was like pulling teeth."

The resident pulled the mask from his face, darting an angry glance in Laurie's direction. "In slow motion," he said.

Laurie busied herself gathering instruments from the tray at her side. She had said "I'm sorry, Doctor" too many times during the operation for the words to have any meaning now. The doctors left without saying a direct word to her.

When the O.R. was cleaned up and ready again for use, Laurie mumbled, "I'll

41

see you in the morning" to the other nurses. Wanting only to run, to go home, to be alone, she was startled by the sharp sound of her superior's voice as she passed Mrs. Hunt's office on her way to the lockers.

"Miss Davis?"

Laurie found herself sitting on the edge of a chair facing the head surgical nurse's desk. She was feeling strangely detached, as though she, like the splenectomy patient, were floating in a deadening cloud of anesthesia.

The fiftyish, finger-drumming little martinet who supervised Laurie's department had a voice that resembled short-wave static, even when she strained to sound sympathetic. "Dr. Bateman is usually very reasonable," she was saying. "Dr. Pelletier, I'll grant you, is extremely edgy. But when the attending *and* the resident complain, my responsibility becomes quite clear, Miss Davis."

Laurie's fingertips pressed into her palms. She raked her mind for a response, but there was nothing she could say; the complaints had been justified. (Would it have helped to tell Ron she loved him, that his future mattered to her more than her own? No. *"Later. I'll see you around."*)

Ron's words mingled, hollow and mocking, with the crackling voice of Mrs. Hunt. "I've always considered you an exceptional instrument nurse, my dear. I can name any number of attendings who'd rather have you on scrub duty than any nurse on my shift. I *must* say, however, that lately you haven't been up to standard. You seem tired. Have you had a complete checkup recently?"

Laurie shook her head, "I'm not . . ."

"You look anemic," the grating voice persisted. "You look positively faint."

Laurie grasped the arms of her chair, forcing herself to attention. "No, I'm all right. Today . . . I'm sorry about what happened today. It won't happen again, Mrs. Hunt."

"I'm afraid I *can't* let it happen again," Mrs. Hunt said. Her Rock-of-Gibraltar face remained expressionless, but her wiry fingers accelerated their tattoo on the desk top. "I don't know how long it's been since you've had a rest, Miss Davis. I think you once told me you worked your way through nursing school? And then you came directly to this hospital after graduation? In six months, apart from one day off every week — Miss Davis, are you all right?"

43

"Maybe a little tired," Laurie admitted. (Why didn't the woman stop talking and let her go home?)

"I don't like doing this, but I'm sure the Supervisor of Nursing Services will agree. If you won't — if you *can't* take time off to get yourself into a . . . calmer state, I'm going to recommend your transfer to another floor."

"But I'm a surgical nurse! I —"

"You're a nurse, period," Mrs. Hunt corrected. "You're trained for general duty. I'm sure that we can find less demanding services for you, at least for a while." She must have noticed the tears welling up in Laurie's eyes, because the crisp intonation became less harsh. "This isn't a punishment or a demotion, Miss Davis. It's certainly no disgrace. I'm merely taking a precautionary measure. For your sake as well as the hospital's. To say nothing of the patients who come here for surgery. In the O.R. there isn't room for the most minute error. There's little enough room for it anywhere in the profession, but I'm hoping that in a less critical job . . ."

There would have been no arguing with Mrs. Hunt even if Laurie had found the strength to argue. Adamant, she instructed Laurie to report to the Supervisor the next morning. Considering the shortage of scrub nurses on the staff, the order added to Laurie's depression. It's that bad, she thought. Can't even tolerate me in the O.R. for one day while they find a replacement.

"Now, cheer up," Mrs. Hunt chirped as Laurie was excused from the office. "You'll be back in surgery soon enough, I'm sure." To punctuate her assurances, she indulged herself in a rare, humorless smile. "It's hardly the end of the world, you know."

It might as well have been, Laurie thought. Though when you lose the two loves in your life in a single afternoon, the end of the world could come and go almost unnoticed.

Four

Exactly two weeks after her transfer from surgery to general duty on the maternity floor (where the head nurse had apparently been cautioned to keep her busy with duties involving no more responsibility than that given to the aides), Laurie came home from the hospital to find a note scribbled by Evelyn Maiwald, one of her apartment mates:

Dreamy-sounding guy called 2:45. Wants you to call him back. If you don't, I will.
E. (for Envious)

Printed underneath, in oversized letters, was an unfamiliar number.

It wouldn't be Ron, of course; he had probably moved out of the dormitory and had a new number, but Evelyn would have recognized his voice. No one she knew at the hospital would call at 2:45, knowing

she was on duty until three. Curiosity over-
came the brooding lethargy that had fallen
over her since the break with Ron. Laurie
dialed, hearing the buzz on the other end
only once before a faintly familiar male
voice responded:

"Hello?"

"This is Laurie Davis. Did someone at
this number . . . ?"

"Yah, *I* did. How's it going, Laurie?"

"Linc Addison?" she guessed.

"That's cheating. You peeked. Tell me,
are you still saving humanity, nine-to-
five?"

"Seven-to-three," Laurie corrected, suddenly irritated.

"Well, don't get upset. It's a minor tem-
poral error. Actually, I was referring to
your life philosophy." Linc sounded inordi-
nately cheerful, brushing off the resentful
edge in Laurie's voice as though oversensi-
tive people who took themselves too seriously weren't to be taken seriously. "No,
what I really want to know is, are you
doing anything spectacular tonight?"

Laurie hesitated. For a moment she had
suspected that Linc had contacted her to
gloat over his "victory," and decided not to
give him the satisfaction of mentioning
Ron's name. In the next instant, she con-

cluded that her thought was worthy of a petty ten year old. And now this bland proof of innocence! It hadn't occurred to Linc that she might be annoyed, because he had never thought they were competing for the right to influence Ron's future.

She must have been silent longer than she supposed. "Laurie? Look, if you're searching for some painless way to tell me to drop dead, don't bother. I know how chicks feel about last-minute invites. Sounds like you were number ninety-seven in my catalog and I've already gone through ninety-six refusals."

Laurie was surprised to find that her laughter was still so close to the surface. "I didn't even think I was listed."

"We-e-ll, this party came up sort of spur-of-the-moment," Linc drawled. "It's at the Barclays' in La Jolla."

"The drugstore Barclays?"

"Right. Eddy's being his usual friendly little self, inviting everybody he sees, so I don't know. Maybe it'll be a ho-dad rockout. But, as I said, if you don't have any sensational plans, be assured — The Great Kahuna called you *first*."

Tactfully, he didn't mention having cleared the invitation with Ron. But the realization that Ron would probably be at

48

Eddy Barclay's party left Laurie with mixed emotions. It would hurt to see him with another girl. Yet, she would see him again, and he wouldn't be feeling sorry for poor old Laurie, because she wouldn't be alone. "I don't know what a ho-dad rockout *is*," she heard herself saying, "but if it *becomes* one, can we leave early?"

"We haven't gone yet and already we're leaving." Linc laughed shortly. "Is that an answer? Do I cruise by for you, say, around eight-thirty?"

"Fine. Do you know where I live?"

"No, I could have asked Tercotte when I got your phone number from him, but that would have been presumptuous. And if there's one thing we Addisons aren't, it's presumptuous. Route me."

Laurie gave him her address and proper directions, and dropped the receiver shortly afterward with mingled feelings of exultation and disappointment. An attractive man, but one who meant nothing to her emotionally, had offered balm for her bruised ego, and an opportunity to be near Ron once again. But Linc had gotten her phone number from Ron, proving one of two things: either Ron, too, was anxious to reestablish contact, or (and this seemed more likely) he didn't care who dated

Laurie because he had completely lost interest.

Eddy Barclay's home was as lavish as he was simple. A two-storied, mammoth structure of glass and what appeared to be volcanic rock, it was cantilevered on heavy steel beams from the ledge of a steep hillside, facing west. By daylight, the transparent walls probably afforded a breathtaking view of the Pacific. The ultramodern structure barely touched ground, except where the curving driveway swept up to its several entrances. Laurie marveled at the architectural genius. "If they ever decide to sell it, they won't be able to advertise a house and lot for sale. There's no *lot!*"

"The way it's rocking, there won't be a house, either." Linc was referring to the thumping of drums and the twang of electric guitars that vibrated from the Barclay residence, topped by the sound of uninhibited young voices.

At the door, Linc glanced back to survey the black-topped parking area, crowded with unconventional vehicles ranging from racy sports cars to a reconverted hearse. The latter, incongruously, was plastered with surfboard manufacturers' insignia decals. There were a number of old wood-paneled station wagons parked at zigzag angles, and Laurie had noticed a few others among the cars lining the private road up the hillside, where Linc had parked his own surprisingly sedate convertible; Ron's "woodie" was not among them.

Swallowing her disappointment, Laurie let herself be guided into a huge terrazzo-floored room, jammed with jumping humanity and already clouded with cigarette smoke. Furniture had either been removed or pushed against the walls to make room for the gyrating couples. A four-piece rock 'n roll combo, manic in movement and Edwardian in haircut, occupied one corner of the room, filling it with an infectious, non-Edwardian beat.

Far across the room, Eddy Barclay, looking like a stranger who had wandered in and obviously didn't belong, waved an enthusiastic welcome, then pushed his way across the floor, avoiding the dancers with awkward halfback maneuvers.

"Hey, wow, Linc. Like, I was wondering if you'd ever get here." Eddy ducked his head at Laurie. "Hi! Man, you look groovy in that dress!" His usually pale face flushed with embarrassment, and Linc came to his rescue:

51

"This is Laurie Davis."

Eddy grinned sheepishly. "I've seen you before, but I didn't know your name. You're *Ron's* girl friend."

Eddy's pleasure at remembering that vital detail was squelched by a weary sigh from Linc.

"What did I say? Did I say the wrong thing?" Their host felt obliged to explain to Laurie, "I always say the wrong thing. Hey, I shouldn't be keeping you here by the door. C'mon in. It's going along pretty great. I *think* it is, anyway. I mean, I didn't think this many guys would show up."

As they were being led across the room they bumped into a shoeless girl who seemed to be enjoying her uninhibited dance, oblivious to the absence of her partner. Eddy paused to apologize profusely, getting in the way of others and earning several scowling looks and someone's growled, "Out of the way, creep." Eddy apologized again. No one would have believed that this fabulous modern castle in the air was his home and that the others were his guests. Most of the couples at the party, Laurie guessed, didn't know Eddy's name and cared even less.

Laurie was remembering one of Ron's appraisals ("Eddy's the kind of klutz who puts the chairs away after a surf club meeting while the other guys go out for beers") when Linc leaned toward her ear, bellowing over the din of the music, "We'll come back here later. I have to see Eddy's folks for a few minutes."

Laurie nodded, not sure that she was anxious to rejoin the bedlam. Every girl in the room looked to be four or five years her junior. She felt overdressed in the emerald green sheath she had been saving for a special occasion, especially since Linc had arrived at her door in slacks and a sweater, and most of the girls present were wearing tight stretch Capris and sleeveless pullovers. Worse still, during the past three and a half years she had been too busy to keep up with the rapidly shifting dance crazes; in this crowd she would look as hopelessly outdated as a flapper out of the Roaring Twenties doing the Charleston.

She felt only slightly more comfortable as she maneuvered the steep, freestanding staircase in her high heels, following Eddy Barclay, with Linc maintaining a protective grip on her arm.

Seconds later, she was being ushered into a smartly furnished sitting room dominated by a monstrous black lava-stone fireplace in which a cheerful blaze crackled. The opposite end of the bleached-mahogany paneled room was sheathed with glass, and framed an impressive picture of a night punctuated by stars and the lights of the town below.

As the trio entered the room, a sleek, sandy-haired man, probably in his late forties, rose from an armchair to greet them. He was close to Laurie's height, and Linc seemed to tower above him. A monogrammed, wine-colored smoking jacket and a wispy, colorless mustache gave him the appearance of an aging roué, and Laurie cautioned herself against surface judgments. Managing a cigar in one hand and a highball glass in the other, he nodded an amiable greeting at Linc and surveyed Laurie with quick-darting, gray-green eyes as Eddy introduced them:

"Ah . . . this is my dad." The boy flushed again, snapping his thick fingers in embarrassment. "Man, I sure fouled that up. You're supposed to say the woman's name first, aren't you?" In his confusion over the proper etiquette, he had evidently forgotten Laurie's name again.

"This is Laurie Davis, Craig," Linc said smoothly.

Mr. Barclay threw a hopeless glance at his son, shifted the cigar to his mouth, and said, "We're delighted to have you, Miss Davis." His eyes swept the contours of Laurie's green dress with disconcerting approval. "Refreshing to see a girl looking like a girl. I had a brief view of some of Eddy's other guests, and frankly, between trousered females and long-haired boys, I would have needed a scorecard to know who's who." Mr. Barclay gestured simultaneously toward a built-in bar and an elongated white couch. "Make yourselves comfortable. I'm drinking Scotch. Can I fix you up?"

Laurie declined politely; Linc was more abrupt. "I'm a milk man, remember?" He dropped into the couch, patting the seat beside him and Laurie sat down, too.

Eddy was left standing near the doorway as Craig Barclay resettled himself in the chair he had been occupying earlier. He started to say something, then turned an annoyed scowl toward his son. "Will you shut that door, Ed? We can't talk with that racket going on downstairs."

Eddy shifted his position nervously. "Maybe I should go back. I mean, I should be keeping the thing going and . . . and all that jazz."

Laurie sensed that he knew the party would not be affected one way or another

55

by his absence, and for the first time she detected an underlying wistfulness beneath the eager tail-waggling puppy-dog facade. Furthermore, Eddy seemed to be more ill at ease around his father than in the company of strangers. He hurried out of the room, obviously relieved, when Mr. Barclay agreed that he should remain with his "friends."

"That's better," the elder Barclay purred when the door was closed. "You say you're a milk man, Linc. I'm a Guy Lombardo waltz man, myself. I'm getting too old to appreciate what passes for music with the new generation." He flashed a not wholly sincere smile at Laurie, and she suspected he was inviting her assurance that he didn't look *that* old. There was no doubt that he devoted time and money to preserving a youthful appearance, though the glass in his hand was a tip-off to the creeping lines of dissipation around his eyes.

Linc ignored the blatant cue for a compliment. "I thought Vivian was going to be in on this meeting."

"She will be. I think she's gone to take another aspirin." From the lower story, the party sounds infiltrated the room, muted now, but still clearly audible. "She's being the martyred heroine tonight. Noise upsets her nerves, but . . ." Mr. Barclay raised his pitch to a mincing and, Laurie felt, vindictive imitation of his wife's voice, ". . . 'We've got to make sacrifices for Eddy's social life. The boy's friends are important too . . .' "

Another door had been opened during the derisive speech. Laurie turned at the sound of a voice not unlike the one Mr. Barclay had been mimicking.

"If that's supposed to be clever, Craig, I'm not at all amused!"

The voice was followed into the room by its owner, a still-handsome, fortyish woman whose gleaming black hair had been tortured into an intricate, high-standing coiffure and lacquered into place. She had the svelte figure of a magazine model, and it was enhanced by a Spanish-styled lounging costume that would have done credit to the flashiest of matadors; the slim black trousers were tighter than any Laurie had seen on the younger set downstairs, and the red velvet jacket looked as though the woman hadn't put it on but had been dipped into it.

She half-tottered, half-swept toward the bar, splashed a liberal dose of amber fluid into a tall ice-filled glass, and carried the drink to a lounge chair near the fireplace. "My apologies, Linc. I didn't mean to ignore you, but my head is splitting and I'm simply not in the mood for Daddy's sick humor."

Mrs. Barclay's tone was even more acid when she referred to her husband than when he had talked about her.

Linc seemed capable of rising above the tension that electrified the atmosphere. "Vivian, this is Laurie Davis. Laurie — Mrs. Barclay."

The woman released a tinny, apologetic laugh. "She's already gotten a splendid introduction to me." To Laurie's sedate, "How do you do?" Mrs. Barclay replied, "I *don't* usually make such witchy entrances, dear. It's not just the infernal noise — I expected to put up with that. But Eddy's been in a swivet all day, worrying that no one would come to his party, and I've worn myself out assuring him that he *does* have scads of friends. He's terribly insecure, and he's had several traumatic experiences. . . ." Mrs. Barclay paused to light a cigarette with shaky, long-nailed fingers, and Laurie noticed that her heavily madeup eyes reflected the same melancholy that had shadowed Eddy's. The eyes were a striking blue-violet color, enlarged by expertly applied artificial eyelashes. They seemed out of balance with Mrs. Barclay's thin, hard-lined mouth. "Really the boy has no confidence in himself at all."

"He's been pushed in the wrong direction," Mr. Barclay insisted. "Any fool can see he's not college material. But mother wants her baby to be an egghead."

Vivian Barclay blew an angry cloud of smoke into the air. "I encouraged him to go to an undemanding junior college. Is that pushing him beyond his . . . ?"

"And he flunked out!" Mr. Barclay made his point as though he had scored a major victory. "Talk about shattering the kid's confidence!"

"Is it unreasonable to want him to get an education? To have him amount to something? You said yourself he'd make a shambles of your business if you took him in!"

"He *would!*"

"Maybe I don't want him stepping into your shoes the way you stepped into *your* father's. You don't even manage the business — you pay people to do your thinking for you. A ready-made success — no initiative required, no imagination, no knowledge, no . . ."

"Go on, say it! 'No guts.' Tell the world

what you think of the poor sucker million-
aire you conned into marrying you. What
were you when I picked *you* up? Second-
row hoofer in a second-rate clip joint,
wearing three spangles and a feather!"

"Craig, I don't have to listen to this!"

Laurie squirmed uncomfortably toward
the edge of the sofa cushion. Linc cleared
his throat meaningfully. During the shrill,
hate-filled exchange, neither of Eddy's parents had taken their captive audience into
account. They were spitting out their
venom in an accelerating rhythm that
made Laurie think that the lines had been
rehearsed, or spewed forth so often that
they sprang to their lips mindlessly and au-
tomatically.

Mr. Barclay was the first to recognize
that the scene had flooded the room with a
humiliating uneasiness. With studied calm,
he drained his glass and said, "There's
nothing to be gained by arguing the matter
anymore, Vivian." He made a dismissing,
chuckling sound, addressing Linc. "Nothing like airing our little family squabbles in
public, eh? My point is — while Viv was
trying to make an intellectual of the boy,
and I was hoping to groom him for a man-
agement position with Barclay Drugstores,
Eddy found his *own* medium. He's a born

surfer, and I say let's get behind him. He's enthusiastic, he seems to have a natural bent for wave riding. . . ."

Eddy's father went on, lauding the boy for abilities he didn't possess, comparing him with some of the big names in the surfing world, and including himself in the plaudits by mentioning that in his younger days he had been "quite an athlete" himself.

Linc's face remained impassive during this pathetic recital. There probably wouldn't be enough profit from his projected film to justify the Barclay investment; Ron had said that. Ron had also said that if any shots were taken of Eddy Barclay, they would be used for comedy relief. Yet Linc was sitting here now, sensibly silent, but undoubtedly squirming inside, listening to Craig Barclay's unrealistic evaluation of Eddy's prowess on a surfboard. Not agreeing with the man, but not disagreeing, either. Linc had "lined up his pigeon," as Ron expressed it. Having heard the Barclays argue, having witnessed their frustration over Eddy's limited potential, Laurie could see that they hoped to buy Eddy's success for him. It was hard to decide who was more deserving of pity — Eddy or his embittered parents.

Linc ended the discussion of Eddy by asking if his sponsor had had time to make a final check of the proposed budget.

"It all sounds reasonable," Mr. Barclay said. He had gotten up to refill his glass during his previous speech, and was sipping at it intermittently, appearing every inch the successful businessman now. Paternal and amused, he noted that "Unforeseen Expenses" and "Miscellaneous" were overlapping items, and that Linc had asked for enough allowance there to account for a major eruption of Maana Loa. "But, as a matter fact, I think you might be a shade low in estimating costs for accommodations." Then, astoundingly, the drugstore heir winked at Laurie. "I'd say his allotment for medical services is fair enough, wouldn't you?"

"I . . . don't know." Bewildered, Laurie glanced over to see that Linc was struggling to contain laughter.

Vivian Barclay rose to trace her husband's path to the bar. "*That* certainly doesn't make sense. If you're coming along as the safari nurse, you'd think these brilliant entrepreneurs would tell you what you can expect in the way of a salary."

"A *salary?*"

Linc enjoyed Laurie's confusion for a

few seconds, and then announced to the Barclays, "I haven't told Laurie we want her yet. After all, I just made you two see the light yesterday. On a safari, someone's always getting clobbered by a board. Or about the time Sunset's running twenty feet, your best big-wave rider will be running a hundred and two with the flu. Not to mention infected coral cuts and those miserable sea urchin spikes that get imbedded in your feet. . . ."

"There's no doubt that we need a nurse," Mr. Barclay said impatiently. "But we assumed — at least *I* did — that you'd already talked to . . ."

"I'll talk to her later," Linc said. He wound up a brief discussion of some minor business details with Eddy's father, and soon afterward, Vivian Barclay was pressing Laurie's hand and saying, "Oh, I *do* hope you'll accept! You can help me chaperone Diane, for one thing. And you'd be such a wonderful influence on Eddy. A nurse! You know, secretly, I've always hoped Eddy would take an interest in becoming a doctor."

Mr. Barclay grunted; he and his wife glared at each other for a moment, and Linc whisked Laurie out of the room.

Downstairs, the party was taking on the

overtones of a modern-day Bacchanalian orgy. Over the clamor, Linc roared, "I was afraid of this. Stupid Eddy. He breezed the word around to every ho-daddy in Southern California. None of these creeps surf. They just hang around the beaches acting like hoods and giving the sport a bad name. Let's split."

Laurie surveyed the destructive bedlam. Ron was not present. And Eddy was vainly trying to restore some semblance of order, ducking a barrage of flying beer cans for his trouble.

When they had shoved their way to the door, Laurie hesitated, frowning her concern. "Shouldn't you try to help Eddy? He looks so helpless, trying to calm those big toughs."

"We'll call the cops from town." Linc shrugged. "The kid's got to learn to use his brains *some* day."

When they had returned to the relative sanity of Linc's car, he said, "I didn't mean to throw you a curve tonight. I thought it only fair to let you meet Craig and Vivian in their natural state before you made a decision."

"Are you . . . are they serious? About hiring me?"

"Certainly we're serious. Don't tell me

you're going to go into a long thing about how badly you're needed at the hospital, and how you couldn't possibly take a soft job that someone cooked up for you. Think about it, girl. A groovy vacation with pay, chance to see the Islands, Australia. . . ."

And to be with Ron Tercotte, Laurie thought. To have him see me at my best — relaxed and having fun on a beautiful beach somewhere. To talk to him — convince him that he's got to go back to school in February.

"Don't be a squirrel," Linc was saying over the purr of the motor. "If you give me one word about sacrificing your pleasure because the operating room can't function without you, I'll . . ."

"The operating room is functioning *very* efficiently without me," Laurie said.

She hadn't told him about her humiliating transfer, or her supervisor's advice about taking a long rest. Linc interpreted her words as an answer. "You mean you're already on the plane. Now you're getting wise, honey. You're going to have a ball."

"I . . . haven't gotten used to the idea yet," Laurie told him. "Pardon me if I act a little dazed. Like forgetting to thank you."

"I have ulterior motives." Linc laughed.

"No, seriously, you won't be superfluous. I could have conned the Barclays into signing on Dracula's daughter, but this job is for real. So feel needed."

"It's one of those fairy-tale things that people dream about, not something that really happens. *Me! I'm* going to fly to Hawaii?"

"In two and a half weeks."

Laurie felt a sudden giddiness, and then a hopeful thought flickered through her mind. "Whose idea was it, anyway? To include me?"

"Mine," Linc said flatly. He did a querulous double take an instant later, throwing a single dark cloud over Laurie's excitement. "I got the idea. Who else?"

Five

Moments after the chartered jet roared skyward from the runway at Los Angeles International Airport, Laurie found herself in the position of a stranger at an exclusive club.

Linc Addison's responsibilities for organizing the safari kept him rushing frantically until the moment of departure, to make certain that cameras, film, surfboards, and surfers were all aboard and accounted for. Once airborne, he busied himself with a sheaf of paper plans, communicating with no one.

Without Linc to ease the way, Laurie felt lost. Linc's selected surfing stars, who answered to names like Goofyfoot, Elephant, Beast, and Preacher, overanimated by enthusiasm, rocked the cabin with noisy hijinks for the first quarter-hour or so, after which they settled down to equally boisterous conversations about "spectacular wipe-outs," "fabulous left slides," and the thrills of being "locked in" or "shooting through the tube" of a remembered wave.

Surprisingly (because Laurie had expected the couple to finance the expedition but not to participate in it), Craig and Vivian Barclay were aboard, alternately sniping at each other or dozing. They had lingered in the airport's cocktail lounge until the last possible minute, and Mrs. Barclay, elegant in a beige suit piped with black, had needed assistance in getting to the plane.

Eddy Barclay, who never looked particularly at ease, reacted to his parents' presence with acute embarrassment. For a while, he wandered up and down the aisle, making futile attempts to become a part of the general camaraderie. Ignored, Eddy plopped himself into the vacant seat beside Laurie, keeping up a steady, if disjointed, monologue. When he had exhausted comments about the weather, the time they were scheduled to arrive in Honolulu, and an explanation of why most of the surfers had taken along two boards (a smaller "hot dogging" board and a big "elephant gun," designed for big-wave riding), Eddy lapsed into a series of the irrelevant, encyclopedic bits of information that newspapers use to fill out a column. Did Laurie know that a shark must keep swimming or it will sink to the bottom of the ocean? Did she know that Mount Waialeale in Hawaii got an annual average of 471 inches of rain? Or that, this year, American farmers expected to produce about 163 million turkeys?

"That's a lot of turkeys," Laurie replied.

Eddy seemed pleased with the inane response. "I like to learn little interesting facts like that," he said proudly. "I mean — say, you meet somebody new and you can't think of anything to talk about. Well, I spring some bit of information that most people don't know, and that way we get to talking. Like, about the turkeys. Usually, I let the person guess. I ask them a question, see, like I'd say to you, 'How many girls have joined the Girl Scouts since 1912?' That's not one of the more interesting bits of data, but take a guess."

Laurie forced herself to look away from the breathtaking expanse of the Pacific below, "Oh . . . nine million?"

"More than double that," Eddy announced triumphantly. "*Eighteen* million, five hundred thousand? See what I mean?"

"That," Laurie commented, "is a lot of Girl Scouts." She hoped Eddy wouldn't regale her with statistical comparisons of

turkey production and scouting enroll-
ments. But for all her boredom with the
subject matter, as she listened to Eddy
Barclay she was overcome by a profound
sorrow that almost matched a more personal misery that had swept over her this
morning. How desperately Eddy craved
approval and interest! Rejected as a "kook"
by his own age group, a disappointment to
his parents (who either bickered over his
lack of talents or forced him into roles he
could never master), he played the clown.
And purposefully collected "data" that
would "open conversations with new
friends," fervently reciting "interesting
facts" that he hoped would win someone's
respect, if not admiration.

Laurie decided to let Eddy shine with his
knowledge of more immediate facts. She
asked him questions about the passengers,
secretly ashamed of the fact that she was
interested in only one, and discreetly
saving the most important question for the
last.

From their seat near the back of the
plane, Eddy gave brief, worshipful biogra-
phies of the surf heroes who occupied the
seats ahead. Tiny Toshi Nomura's home
was in the Islands; his favorite sport, next
to surfing, was pretending he could speak

only pidgin English. That older, enormous hulk of a character next to Toshi, the one called simply "Beast," looked, acted, and talked, when he talked at all, like a retarded leftover from the Neolithic age. But he held a Ph.D. from Stanford and, though he replied to most questions in guttural grunts, was known to be fluent in Greek, French, Hebrew and two Chinese dialects, not to mention the most exotic language of all — American Surfese.

"Goofyfoot" was described as a "fantastically funny guy," though, judging from Eddy's description of this wag's devastatingly hilarious practical jokes, Laurie classified him as a sadistic moron.

She found herself growing tense as Eddy's catalog of personalities approached Ron. Eddy dismissed Ron with the attitude of an M.C. introducing a celebrity so well known that he needs no introduction. "Anyway, you know him. In fact, I was kind of surprised to —" Eddy's face reddened. "Here I go. Sayin' the wrong thing again."

Laurie saved him from chagrin by pretending she didn't understand. "You haven't said anything wrong."

"No? Oh. Well, I started to say, I was surprised to see you sitting alone. I guess none of the other guys came over at first because they'd seen you at the beach with Ron. I guess it's not serious or anything, huh?"

Laurie assured him that her relationship was not "serious or anything."

"Yeah. Come to think of it, you came to my party with Linc." Eddy was diverted from further conjecture about Laurie's romantic life. His grasshopper mind had leaped back to the debacle of his party. "Man, was *that* a mess! All the wrong people came. Guys I shouldn't have invited, and a bunch of crashers I never saw before. Beer cans all over the place, and broken bottles all over the bottom of the pool. They wrecked a lot of furniture, and one cat threw a marble-top table through one of the big glass walls. It got all out of control and, man, was I scared! In a way, because of my folks, I hated to see the cops. But I was glad they came and broke it up."

Linc should have stayed and helped him, Laurie thought fleetingly. Looking around her, she had the impression that all of the young men aboard were alike in that one respect; perhaps they weren't completely selfish — for all she knew, they did favors for each other and were generous with their time and money within their own surfing society. But she sensed a peculiar snobbishness among them. They were the elite; they seemed to exist primarily for their own pleasure, and the more an outsider like Eddy Barclay accommodated them, the more contempt they showed for him. Linc had let Eddy struggle his way out of a bad situation alone; Ron hadn't even honored Eddy's invitation with his presence.

Cool, she was thinking. Poised, self-assured, unconcerned. Ron, seeing her at the airport this morning, had raised his hand to make a slow half-circular gesture of greeting and had said, "Hi, Laurie. I *heard* you were going to make this scene. Crazy." Said that as blandly as if he were saying good morning to an elevator man he saw every day and wouldn't miss if he never saw again!

In that moment, the days of anticipation and the hours of planning and preparation seemed to melt into an icy pool of disappointment. It had all been wasted — her careful purchase of the pale blue knit suit that had cost more than a week's salary, the frantic last-minute appointment at the hairdresser's last night, the sleepless hours after that, the strict instructions to herself about how to behave when she met Ron (*Let him know you're glad to see him, but don't act like you've been crying yourself to sleep over him!*). It had all been a waste of time.

Worse still, while she had been framing a deceptively nonchalant response to his greeting, Ron had introduced her to the girl who was sharing his plane seat — a petite, golden-skinned girl with huge hazel eyes that were set in a delicate-featured pixie face. Her dark, curling hair was cut short and had that enviable quality of looking as though she didn't care how it looked, but it just *happened* to appear chic. Ron pronounced her name, Diane Etheridge, as though it were a venerated title, and the girl had nodded in response to Laurie's name with the regal disdain of a queen acknowledging the existence of one of her less desirable subjects.

Well, no . . . to be fair, Diane Etheridge had smiled, and maybe it was only jealous resentment that made the smile seem aloof and somewhat superior. Besides, the girl apparently divided people into only two classes — those who surfed and those who didn't. And the beautiful hazel eyes had examined Laurie with a mixed amusement and pity when Ron had said, "Laurie's just

74

coming along as our nurse."

Now, with Ron engaged in animated chatter with the attractive and unexpected female member of the safari, and with misery sitting like a leaden weight on Laurie's chest, Eddy Barclay said, "Diane hasn't ever won any contests, but that's only because she never entered any. Linc rates her as one of the top girl surfers. Man, she and Ron ought to clean up in the tandem events at Makaha."

"Tandem? Is that . . ."

"Two on a board," Eddy explained. "The guy holds the girl in all kinds of fancy poses — over his head and all that jazz. They'll have to work together a lot more to perfect their style, but they're fantastic together. Like Linc says — a natural team."

Laurie nodded glumly. And, suddenly, it came to her that she was as much a misfit in this company as the oddly likeable kid at her side. Misfits need each other's company, but she no longer wanted to hear all there was to know about Diane Etheridge. With only a little encouragement, Eddy was switched to a less depressing line of conversation.

Five hours later, with the islands glistening below like emeralds in a turquoise setting, the young man whose disgruntled parents had made this trip possible for everyone aboard was saying, "And another interesting thing most people don't know about the albatross. It can fly 60 miles an hour. People are always surprised when I tell them. I'll bet you didn't know that, did you, Laurie?"

They were approaching their landing strip at Honolulu International Airport. Looking down, grateful for the opportunity to turn her face away from Eddy's view, Laurie said, "I guess there are lots of things I don't know."

Six

Linc Addison's genius for organization included having two rented houses ready for the group at Sunset Beach, where the sight and sound of spectacular waves compensated for whatever posh appointments the Barclays might have missed.

The larger of the two flat-roofed frame structures served as quarters for Ron, Toshi Nomura, Beast, and most of the other surfers; within hours the front yard was festooned with sandy boards, wet swim trunks, fresh pineapples, beer cans, and guitars.

The "Executive Mansion" was a smaller house next door. Here, the Barclays occupied one bedroom; Linc and Eddy used another as a combination office, photo-equipment warehouse and sleeping room. Laurie found herself sharing the third bedroom with Diane Etheridge.

Neither Diane nor Laurie raised any objection to being roommates, since the arrangement seemed entirely logical. However, there was no enthusiasm on either side, and although Laurie made several attempts to establish a friendly rapport, swallowing her envy of the attention Diane claimed from Ron, she may as well have beamed her personality at a concrete dam. Diane's response to most statements was a wide-eyed stare. In her more exuberant moments, she murmured a deliberately disinterested, "Oh, really?"

By the fifth day, Laurie decided that complete silence was preferable to that cool response; she decided she would address Diane first only under emergency circumstances. If she noticed that Diane's hair was on fire, or if Maana Loa blew itself to bits and hot lava threatened the room, she might casually mention the fact to Diane, Laurie decided.

Fortunately, the shared room was used only after both girls were too exhausted to do anything but sleep. Diane's days were crowded with expeditions, in rented cars, to various beaches. On several mornings, Linc and his surfing stars were gone before Laurie woke up, leaving her with the battling Barclays for company. (Apparently Sunset, at the moment, was "unsurfable," and films were being shot at nearby Haleiwa and other chosen spots. Then too, Linc didn't seem to think that the safari nurse was needed on location.) But if she was forced to listen, by day, to the domestic trials and tribulations of Eddy's parents, each of whom used her as a reluctant confidante, the evenings erased Laurie's sense of being left out.

After the "evening glass-off," when there were no more rides in prospect, surfboards were abandoned for other pleasures. There were sumptuous dinners served on the porch of the Executive Mansion by a grinning Chinese cook, nicknamed Gaston Escoffier by the surfers. Although there was no time to cover the usual tourist sights, one evening Linc arranged for a giant luau in the exotic, orchid-bedecked garden of a luxury hotel. And as the Christmas holidays approached, and more and more suffers arrived from the mainland for the International contest, the larger house echoed every night with recorded rock 'n roll music, ebullient laughter, and wave-oriented conversation.

During these informal parties, Laurie began to enjoy as much attention as the girl who spoke the suffers' language, but the reason for her popularity wasn't encouraging; when Diane wasn't surfing with Ron, she was dancing or strolling along the beach with him. Diane had no time for other men, thus leaving the field free for Laurie. It was a depressing way to eliminate the only competition.

Linc, when he wasn't shooting surf film, or surfing himself, was fiddling with his camera equipment or checking out the innumerable details of transportation and housing that still lay ahead. But what time he had to spare was spent with Laurie. He was seated beside her one evening at the dinner table, after Ron, Diane, and a few of the others had wandered off. While they dawdled over Gaston's coffee, which was just barely distinguishable from tea, Beast, Goofyfoot, and Toshi had launched one of their poker-faced teasing attacks on Eddy Barclay.

"Tell the other guys," Goofyfoot was saying. "You know, Eddy . . . that thing you told me a while ago. . . ."

Eddy's face had turned to a blushing rose color, probably because he suspected he was being ridiculed. Yet Goofyfoot sounded utterly sincere, and the others were showing rapt interest. "You mean, about . . . Christmas trees?"

Goofyfoot nodded. "Yeah. Listen to this,

fellas — this is fascinating! Like, we're talking about putting a Christmas tree up on our porch, and right out of thin air Eddy comes out with this interesting and appropriate piece of information."

Beast shook his head from side to side in feigned awe. "He's constantly doing that."

"He's a veritable gold mine of encyclopedic facts," Goofyfoot agreed.

"Head belong him plenty shopp," Toshi added in the phoney pidgin he affected in front of the Barclays.

"*Tell* them," Goofyfoot urged.

Eddy looked unbearably miserable. "I only said . . . the custom of having Christmas trees was introduced into the U.S. by. . . ."

Beast leaned over the table expectantly. "By *whom?*"

"Listen," Eddy protested. "You guys are puttin' me on!"

"No, we're not. Everybody doesn't *know* these things." Goofyfoot leaned over to whip a ball-point pen from Linc's shirt pocket. "You got something to write on, anybody? I wanna jot this down so I don't forget."

Toshi's long-nailed fingers extracted an envelope from the pocket of his Bermuda

81

shorts. "Here you stay, bruddah. Pants belong lettah."

"Thanks, Tosh. Okay, now, Eddy." Pen poised, Goofyfoot stared at Eddy with knit-browed concentration.

"Well — the name was Reverend Henry Schwahn."

"Spell that."

"S-C-H-W-A-H-N."

"Okay." Goofyfoot scrawled the name on the envelope, whispering audibly, "Reverend S-C-H-W-A-H-N. *Henry.*"

"What year was that?" Beast asked, making it sound like a matter of grave importance.

Eddy gulped. "Eighteen fifty-one." Although convinced by now that he was being made fun of, he apparently couldn't resist adding, "This was in Cleveland, Ohio."

"Can you imagine that?" Goofyfoot folded the envelope carefully and handed it to Toshi. "Can you imagine anybody *knowing* that?"

"*Eddy* knew it."

"Dees fella talk da kine."

They were going along in the same exaggerated vein when Linc muttered, "Okay, the bit's worn out, you cats. Cool it."

They made a production number of

leaving the table, pretending to be over-whelmed by Eddy's display of erudition. Laurie could still hear their voices as they crossed the lawn toward their own quarters. They were in hysterics, and the laughter was heard by Eddy and his parents as well.

"When are you going to stop making an idiot of yourself?" Craig Barclay growled. He ground his cigar dead in an ashtray, shaking with anger. "How you can sit there like an oaf —"

"Leave him alone, Craig!" Vivian Barclay almost snarled the words at her husband. "They give him a bad enough time without you picking him apart!"

Mr. Barclay's fist crashed down to the table. "If you'd stop mollycoddling him, babying him, putting on this big protective act —"

"Stop yelling at me!" Vivian shrieked.

Eddy had gotten up and hurried to his room, but he couldn't have helped hearing his father shout, "How do you expect me to make a man out of him? He's got to learn to defend himself. Why do you think I'm spending all this money — so that he can be a laughingstock?"

Linc had gotten to his feet, signaling for Laurie to join him. Sickened by the scene,

Laurie needed no urging, but as they started toward the outside door, Craig Barclay turned to Linc. "Make him get out there and show some guts, Linc. He's been sitting on the beach since we're here."

"Get out in *that?*" Linc's head gestured toward the surf. The monstrous waves weren't visible in the evening darkness, but the savage pounding of water could be heard even over the Barclays' loud voices. "Craig, he's trying. In two-, three-foot surf he's . . . coming right along. But you'd have to have rocks in your head to let him tackle Sunset."

"It'd make a man out of him." Craig was putting on a "manly" act himself, lighting a fresh cigar.

"Correction," Linc said. It was the first time Laurie had seen him shaken by anger. "Correction. It'd make a drowned kid out of him."

Vivian Barclay had started to sob, and as Linc ushered Laurie out of the house, Eddy's mother was wailing accusations through her tears: "You'd be willing to kill him! Just because you're a nothing . . . you'd let my child drown to prove you're the father of a hero!"

Laurie shuddered, hearing the argument through Eddy's ears. It wasn't until she and Linc had walked to the beach that she stopped trembling. Laurie sank down to the sand and let the hammering surf wash the shrill voices out of her mind. "They fill the air with poison, don't they?" Laurie released a long breath. "They were at it all afternoon, but at least Eddy wasn't around to hear it."

"Must be rough on you," Linc admitted. "From now on, come along with us when we go out."

And watch Ron, Laurie thought dejectedly. Eat my heart out watching Ron frolic around in the water with the hazel-eyed sphinx. No, thank you.

"Did you hear me?" Linc asked. "I'd like having you around, anyway. So would Eddy."

"I don't know which would be worse," Laurie said. "Listening to the Barclays fighting and then crying on my shoulder, or hearing those smart apes torment Eddy that way. Couldn't you get them to act civil, Linc? That business back at the house just now — that was just plain cruel."

"They come on a little strong," Linc admitted. "But Eddy asks for it."

"He has problems."

"Oh, come off it."

"Linc, you *know* he's maladjusted! Look at the way he's been raised — all torn apart with nothing but hostility around him . . ."

"Hey, hold it, honey. I'm shooting a surf film — not running a psychological counseling service."

"Do you have to get paid to show a little human compassion? Where I come from, we try to help someone who's in a rough spot. Everyone here seems to think it's a clue to grind Eddy deeper into the mire."

In the dim light, with only the boiling surf and a handful of newly risen stars visible, Linc's hand managed to find Laurie's and she didn't draw it away. "Let's compromise," Linc said. "I'll see what I can do about inaugurating 'Be Kind to Eddy Barclay Week,' and you start realizing that the world has always had its share of sad sacks."

"I know that, but —"

"And you can waste your life trying to straighten them out, but you won't make it. Five, ten years from now, Eddy's still going to be doing stupid things. Craig and Vivian, if they aren't divorced or they don't kill each other first, will still be snarling at each other. Meanwhile, you can either wear yourself out trying to solve their impossible problems, or . . ." Linc used his grip on Laurie's hand to pull her closer, casually folding her in his arms and brushing his lips against her temple. "Or, you can enjoy the place, the day, the minute, the sensation."

Laurie's body had stiffened, though the embrace, at the moment, had purely brotherly overtones. "Is that what you're doing, Linc? Enjoying the place, the minute . . . ?"

"And the company," he said. "I'm an admitted hedonist. An unselfish form of religion, actually. While the allegedly pious people are getting down on their knees and whining 'gimme, gimme, gimme,' Addison shows his gratitude for what already *is* by enjoying it to the hilt."

Laurie laughed at the incongruous reference to piousness. "Saint Addison."

"Yes, that sounds better than Saint Lincoln, doesn't it? Look, I could talk about my theory all evening, but you still wouldn't understand the live-now bit. Relax. Let me demonstrate. . . ."

Before Laurie could protest, his lips were pressed against hers in a lingering, expert kiss. She began by resisting, but as Linc lifted his head and whispered, "Is this so terrible? Relax!" she found herself responding to the pleasurable sensation.

Linc was, after all, an exceptionally attractive man — physically appealing, mentally stimulating. Did it make sense to spend her evenings brooding about someone who obviously didn't care for her, probably never had and never would? Ron was a glamorous route to spinsterhood. Not that she deluded herself that this moment had any deep emotional meaning for Linc Addison. But he had a point. The night was balmy; in a short while the moon would appear between graceful palm fronds. And this little sand strip between the mountains and the sea was, for now, her whole world. If she failed to enjoy the moment, wishfully remembering the past or daydreaming about the future, could she truly say that she was alive *now?*

When Linc released her, Laurie was breathing hard. "See what I mean?" he asked. He chucked her under the chin playfully. "It's possible to enjoy being kissed by a guy who has no intentions, honorable or otherwise — even when you imagine you're hopelessly in love with another guy."

"Who said I was?"

"Please. No coy denials. Saint Addison, among his other profuse talents, is also an eagle-eyed observer of the human scene."

Laurie was quiet for a moment. "All right. It's either very obvious or you're an extremely astute observer."

"Both," Linc said. "What's more, you're probably enjoying your tortured martyrdom. Women in love have a way of wallowing in their agony."

"I'm not enjoying it and I'm not wallowing." To save face, Laurie forced a facetious laugh. "Keep an eye on your cute little protegée. She just may get her pretty eyes scratched out."

"Wrong approach," Linc advised. "Why not use her tactics?"

"And get surf bumps on my knees? No, I'm afraid she has me outclassed there. I'm not about to take up surfing."

"No, you'd probably go at it so seriously, you'd make Ron look like a gremmie in a few months. That's not what I meant."

"Change my brand of soap?"

"I'm being sensible. Look, Diane's greatest charm for Ron is . . . she isn't trying to direct his life. She has fun with him — she doesn't go around sounding like his mother."

"I sound like his mother?"

"Any time you tell a man what's good for him, he's going to run for the hills. You had Psych in college — I'm surprised you aren't as hip as Diane. She's liable to tie him down for life, but he won't know he's being roped. He thinks he's chasing *her*."

Laurie weighed the oversimplified advice for a few seconds. "I had *child* psychology, Linc. *Children* resent having someone point out a sensible course. *Kids* live for the moment and damn the consequences. And heaven knows, they'd rather play than work."

"Touché, Miss Davis. I take that personally, and I'm wounded."

"You're at least making a career out of your sport. Matter of fact, you work *hard*."

"Ah, you've noticed that."

"But Ron's a born doctor. And when I think of him throwing all that over for —"

"— for the gospel according to Saint Addison, it burns you. Well, remember what I told you about the Barclay tribe. Pair of lushes with a kooky kid. Waste of your time. Guy who's hung up on waves — same thing. Save your time and put your energy to more enjoyable uses."

Linc had reached for her again, when the sound of crunching footsteps interrupted his move. He peered toward the dimly outlined approaching figure, groaning aloud when he saw it was Eddy.

Laurie identified the intruder at the

same time and whispered, "Be nice to him, Linc. He must be feeling awfully low."

A few seconds later, Eddy, apparently blissfully unaware of the old adage about three being a crowd, was saying, "Hey, how *neat!* This is a break — you go for a walk and you run into your two best friends."

Linc muttered something unintelligible under his breath, but Laurie, convinced that the jovial attitude was a coverup for Eddy's depression, assured him that he was welcome.

It was a toss-up, she decided later, whether wrestling with Linc and with her conscience would have been easier than sitting on a romantic beach and watching the new moon rise, while a jolly falsetto voice informed you that automobile thefts had doubled in the past ten years and that ("This is a really interesting thing that most people don't know!") a course in garbage-collecting and disposal was being offered by Rutgers University in New Brunswick, N.J.

Seven

Four days before Christmas, Eddy Barclay managed to win new honors for himself, including titles like "The North Shore Noodlehead," and "The All-Time Wipeout." Furthermore, he gave Laurie her first legitimate excuse for accompanying the safari.

The day began with great promise; Sunset's titanic waves were apparently shaped to perfection for the bigwave riders like Ron, Toshi and Beast, but, as always, too menacing for the "hot dogging" crowd. This meant riders like Goofyfoot and Diane, whose tricky performances called for less killing surf. As a result, Laurie had the pleasure of seeing Diane join the carload headed for Haleiwa Beach, about twelve miles away. Linc was equally relieved to rid himself of his bungling "camera assistant"; Eddy was reluctantly accepted as one of the departing group.

When he filmed rides in less formidable surf, Linc sometimes paddled out on his board, or swam out with a camera encased in a waterproof housing. Here, where paddling out through the spitting giants meant climbing vertical green walls, Linc contented himself with planting his tripod on the beach and shooting with a telephoto lens. Laurie, grateful that Vivian and Craig Barclay were back at the house, evidently sleeping off a hangover, began to experience and understand the fervid enthusiasm that had seized Linc and his camera subjects.

"Look at those sets!" Linc shouted. "What a fantastic lineup! I'm stoked out of my mind!"

Several times, Laurie found herself frozen by fear as Ron disappeared into the hollow tunnel of a pouring monster that blotted out the horizon. But then she saw him, crouched on his board as it shot through the tube, emerging into the sunlight like a sea god being born. There was a breathless moment when Ron's timing was off, or the wave failed to behave as he had judged it would, and he was forced to ditch his board and swim shoreward through the vicious rip. In another wipeout, terrifying minutes dragged by after he dropped through space in a twenty-foot free fall to the inky trough of black water below, tons of angry surf crashing over his head. Again, the exhausting swim through a boiling cauldron of insane water. And then Ron, after retrieving his board, was paddling out once more.

"He's not going back *again?*" Laurie cried incredulously.

From under the black hood that covered his head and camera while he changed film, Linc said, "Of *course* he's going back. Man, did you see him take off on that peak a while ago — that hair-raiser? And then get himself caught again in the inside lineup?"

"I'm impressed," Laurie admitted. "But those waves look so *powerful!* Isn't he — aren't they pushing their luck?"

"You do that every time you drive out on a freeway," Linc told her. "The only difference is, when you get out of your car you're bushed. When it looks like it's going to close out, these guys are going to come back on the beach feeling ten feet tall."

The threatening "close out," when waves lost all semblance of a predictable shape, and the surf became a murderous mass of savage white water, came shortly afterward. Linc accompanied the other members of his group to the house, all of them raving about classic rides and memorable wipeouts, about dropping back "over the falls" and experiencing sensations of dropping through a trap door. Miraculously, Ron lingered behind. For the first time since the safari began, Laurie found herself completely alone with him.

While Ron blotted himself with a towel, they exchanged a few comments about the exceptional footage Linc had gotten for his film this morning. Awkwardly, Laurie admitted that she understood how the thrill of conquering steep, fast, and mammoth waves might become addictive. Ron dropped beside her on the sand. "After a morning like this, it's like a patient coming out of ether. He's been scared to death, but now it's over — and, wow, that knowledge that he's *alive!*"

Laurie smiled. "That's a weird analogy."

"What — the medical bit?" Agreeably, Ron said, "All right, let's try another one. Surgeon coming out of an O.R. after a successful operation."

"Where the odds were stacked against him. I've seen that happen time and again, Ron." She was about to tell him something she had read in one of the surfing magazines Eddy had strewn all over the house.

It was an account of an interview with an exceptionally good surfer who was, first and foremost, a gifted surgeon. Or to tell Ron of hearing that a group of doctors at the Kaiser Hospital right here in Hawaii kept their boards handy and surfed during coffee breaks. But Linc Addison's warning stirred in her mind. Why send Ron "running for the hills" with loaded suggestions? Why repel him by sounding like a not-too-subtle mother handing out sugarcoated advice?

Laurie fell into a dismal silence, combing her mind for something sprightly and arresting to say, something that would keep Ron here at her side. This was the rare moment she had waited for, hoped for, yet she sensed that Ron was getting restless, probably wishing he had gone back with his friends to enjoy a verbal rehash of the morning's triumphs.

Surprisingly, Ron stretched out, wriggling his shoulders into the sand and staring up at the sky, his bronzed face relaxed in what Laurie decided must be a blissful reminiscence of the past few hours.

"I'm beginning to appreciate your outlook," Laurie said. "This certainly beats doing scut work at the hospital."

Ron opened one eye to survey her warily.

"You don't even surf."

Laurie shrugged, pleased with the initial result of her reverse psychology. "No, but I like the beach. I like to swim. I'm enjoying loafing."

Ron raised his head, propping it with his forearm. "Don't forget deals like this are few and far between. I'll bet this is the first film safari that ever rated a full-time nurse."

"Oh, there are other rich people besides the Barclays. I might line up a job as a companion to someone who travels. Maybe light nursing duties . . ."

"With the nursing shortage so serious?" Ron scowled. Then, probably because he realized that the critical question must have sounded absurd coming from him, he modified it by adding, "I mean — from *your* point of view, it's not a very logical plan."

"Points of view can change," Laurie said carelessly. "You're a perfect example. You must have wanted to be a doctor at one time. You changed your mind. Well — other people can see the merits in living for themselves, too."

She hadn't intended to carry the ridiculous thoughts that far, but Laurie was heartened by Ron's reaction.

"You've been talking to Linc," he said.

"A lot of what Linc preaches makes sense." Laurie sensed a vague annoyance on Ron's part, and the conversation was beginning to shape up so that Ron might soon be arguing against the very philosophy that had separated them in the first place. At least, he had launched a speech on why the live-for-today theory might be right for *some* people, but not necessarily for people with Laurie's conditioning, when the discussion was shattered by the unexpected appearance of Goofyfoot. Breathless, he had two things to report: he had just driven past the Banzai Pipeline, a challenging big-wave spot where Linc hoped to get some of his most exciting footage. "The shape-up is terrific. Linc wants to know if you and Toshi are surfed out, or do you want to ride some more?" Almost as an afterthought, Goofyfoot explained that he had come back from Haleiwa early because there'd been an accident.

Laurie scrambled to her feet. "What happened?"

"Oh, it's no big sweat," Goofyfoot assured her. "Diane wiped out and she was body surfing back in to get her board. Just as she came whamming over on the wave, what's there to greet her? Helpful Eddy.

He's straddling his own board and pulling Diane's over to her like a boy scout, like she couldn't get it for herself. Right in her way!"

It was Laurie, not Ron, who asked if Diane had gotten hurt badly.

"Not bad. Don't ask me why; she came down like if you threw a log on a lumber pile. Her ankle's all swollen and she's calling Eddy every name under the sun."

Laurie had already started across the sand, the others trailing her. "What about Eddy?"

Goofyfoot laughed. "Lucky for him, he got hit on the head, where he can't get hurt. The boards went flying like toothpicks. One of the skegs clipped him right about here." Goofyfoot indicated his left temple. "I don't think that's bothering him as much as the way Diane's chewing him out. She can't walk — I had to carry her to the wagon."

Ron shook his head. "I don't blame her for being mad. If she can't stand, it's a cinch she can't enter the Makaha contest." He snapped his fingers. "There goes my partner for the tandem event." Although Ron's seeming indifference should have encouraged Laurie, she was disturbed by the callousness that was exhibited by his next, more concerned question, "You say Pipeline looks boss, huh?"

"El perfecto," Goofyfoot assured him. "Hey, I hear you really turned on this morning. With Linc grindin' away, making every ride immortal?"

During the short walk to the Executive Mansion, they compared notes on the waves they had caught that morning, as though Laurie's reason for hurrying was of no interest to them at all.

As Laurie walked onto the porch of the smaller house, Diane, half-reclining in a lounge chair, was a far cry from her usual super-cool self. "I've waited all year for Makaha!" she was moaning. "If I can't ride, I'll put a board between that stupid gremlin's eyes!"

Linc tried to remind her that Eddy had only tried to be helpful, but Diane was in no mood to be pacified. Furthermore, she was furious with Linc, demanding, "Why can't you or Ron drive me to the hospital?"

Linc refused to get excited, explaining with exaggerated patience, "Because we've got to split for Pipeline. Besides, the Barclays were going shopping in Honolulu anyway."

"Well, just make sure *she's* going, too,"

Diane seethed. "I'm not getting into a car alone with that potbellied wolf."

Diane was giving out vociferous opinions of the Barclays, father and son, as Linc caught sight of Laurie. "Come on over and have a peek at the patient, nursie."

Diane shot Linc a look that said she had no faith in Laurie's ability, but she held still while Laurie examined her swollen ankle.

Anxious to be on his way, but aware of his responsibility, Linc pressed for an opinion. "What say, Laurie? If it's just a sprain, you lay on a little mysto first aid and save the kid a trip. It's probably not —"

"I wouldn't dismiss it too lightly," Laurie said. "It's liable to be more serious than a sprain."

Diane groaned, more in anger than in pain. "Oh, groovy!" She acted as though Laurie had been responsible for her condition. "What does that mean?"

"It means we ought to get you to a doctor. He'll want to take an X ray. Let me slip something over my suit and I'll go with you."

"Never mind," Diane ordered. "Just get me my white beach coat from the room." She glared at Linc. "I don't want people knocking themselves out for me!"

101

On her way to the bedroom, Laurie nearly ran into the Barclays. Craig's new, glaringly touristy Hawaiian print shirt and Vivian's skin-tight wraparound of the same flowered fabric gave them a deceptive appearance of "belonging together." In addition, they looked like an aging showgirl and her shifty-eyed agent about to go out on the town together. Laurie nearly precipitated another explosion between them by asking about Eddy.

"He's locked himself in his room," Vivian whined. "I want him to come to the doctor's with us, but he insists it's just a scratch."

"It probably *is* just a scratch," Craig said through a poisonous cloud of cigar smoke. In a confidential tone, he said to Laurie, "She's always made a big production number out of it. Every time her baby bruised his finger."

"He's embarrassed," Eddy's mother insisted. "That's why he doesn't want anyone to see him. Please have a look at him, Laurie. I'll be so nervous, I won't —"

"She won't be able to enjoy spending my money," Craig muttered. "Oh, come on, let's get that girl to a doctor. First thing you know, I'll have a suit on my hands."

"You see the way he thinks?" Vivian shrilled. "You heard him. He doesn't care about his own son. He's worried about —"

"Will you for once shut up, Vivian? Linc's going to shoot some more film and he probably wants Eddy to get in there and do his stuff." They were on the porch, and Craig Barclay addressed himself to Linc. "Isn't that right? You want to get a few shots of Eddy riding — what's that place you're going to? The Banzai what?"

"Pipeline," Laurie heard Linc reply. "No, actually, Craig, I want to save Eddy for some spectacular sequences at Waikiki."

In spite of her painful injury, Diane's laughter echoed through the house. It was malicious laughter; Craig Barclay was apparently ignorant of the fact that Waikiki's small waves, jammed with rank beginners and paunchy tourists on rented boards, had earned it the surfers' contemptuous nick-name: The Lumber Pile. But though Linc's facetious insult went over Craig's head, it had undoubtedly been heard behind the door of the room in which Eddy had closeted himself.

Laurie gulped down her disgust with all of them as she waited in the living room until the Barclays had gotten Diane to one

103

of the rented station wagons and roared off. Linc didn't return to the house; he was in too great a rush to round up his big-wave stars and take off for the treacherous but exciting Pipeline. No one stopped to ask about Eddy Barclay.

It took masterful persuasion, and an assurance that everyone else had gone, to get Eddy to unlock his door. When he did, Laurie sucked in a shocked breath. The cut, running vertically down the side of his left temple, was not deep. But the surfboard, hurled out of control by a wave, must have landed against his head with a tremendous impact. The skin had been broken, probably by the board's sharp fin, but Laurie was more concerned about a possible internal injury.

"It's no big deal," Eddy insisted as Laurie followed him into the room.

"You should have gone with your folks," Laurie said. "A blow like that to the head . . ."

"I'm okay, honest." Eddy flopped across his bed. "I'm not even dizzy. I was sort of — what I mean is, I actually saw stars for a while there, but —" He kept his face turned away from Laurie, his voice more quavery than usual. "I guess everybody's really burned about the way I loused Diane up. I don't blame her. If I was good enough to get seeded into the finals at Makaha and somebody racked me up so I couldn't enter, I'd . . ."

"Eddy, will you stop apologizing for being alive?"

The sharpness of Laurie's tone brought Eddy's head around. In the bright sunlight pouring in from the window, the gash on his temple gave him a gruesome appearance. His eyes, Laurie noticed, were puffy and red-rimmed, and there were splotches of blood on his white swim trunks.

"Will you start thinking of yourself for a change, the way everyone else around here does?" Unaccountably, Laurie's anger and the selfishness of the others extended itself to Eddy, though for the opposite reason. "Nobody respects a doormat. You were doing Diane a favor. You didn't know she'd come crashing down on you."

"It's still my fault." Eddy sat up, his hands going toward his head in a despondent gesture.

"Don't touch that cut!" More gently, Laurie said, "Let me at least get it cleaned and put a dressing on it."

Eddy argued, probably in the hope that a stoic dismissal of his injury would make him appear more "manly." But he suc-

105

cumbed to Laurie's insistence, and minutes later, when the wound was painted with iodine, Laurie secured a sterile gauze covering with adhesive tape. She was starting to move away from the edge of the bed when Eddy's hand reached out, his thick fingers touching Laurie's wrist hesitantly.

"Laurie?"

She remained motionless, instinct warning her not to reject the timid touch, yet intuitively knowing what was coming next.

"Laurie, you're the only person I know who really understands me. You don't think I'm just a dumb klutz. I mean — you're always so nice, and we get along so great."

"Of course we do, Eddy. You're a wonderful person. If you'd just . . ." Laurie hesitated. It was neither the time to build or to tear down Eddy's confidence in himself.

He had removed his fingers from her arm, but now he was looking at her with a heartbreakingly sincere appeal that would have bordered on the comic if Laurie had been unfamiliar with the boy's tragic need. "Ever since I met you, I've been thinking . . . she can do a lot better than me, but . . . I mean, since we get along so great, and you're always so nice to me, and we're interested in the same things, like unusual facts that most other people don't know about, and . . ." He had evidently mustered up all of his nerve to get this far. Now, as though a dam inside him had burst, Eddy blurted out, "I love you. I really do. Honest, Laurie, I —"

He must have read the pity in her eyes, because the realization shone in his own, moist and pain-filled. Eddy spared her the necessity of explaining that she appreciated his friendship, but her kindness was only that — kindness, and nothing more.

"I guess you're nice to everybody," Eddy croaked. "Not me, 'specially. Everybody." He got to his feet, swayed unsteadily, and dropped back to the bed. He made a joke of it. "I guess I got clobbered harder than I thought. Maybe I'm delirious, huh? Talkin' out of my head?"

"You're not delirious," Laurie assured him. "But you should rest. We'll talk some other time."

"No, it's okay. I said enough." Eddy had turned away from her again. "I think maybe I'll catch me a little nap, like you said."

He was only pretending to be asleep a few seconds later, as Laurie started toward the door. As she passed the desk that separated Eddy's bed from Linc Addison's, Laurie paused, her attention caught by an open, looseleaf notebook. Under a pencil-scrawled heading that read "Conversation Openers with New Friends," Eddy had pasted a series of short "fillers" clipped from newspapers. Guiltily, she took time to read one, tears springing to her eyes at the thought of Eddy hoping to erase his gnawing loneliness by recalling a notice that read: "Marat. Morocco plans a fat-rendering facility."

She left the room, closing the door behind her quietly. She was no more anxious to let Eddy see her face than he was anxious to let Laurie see his.

Eight

Eddy Barclay's only defense was a clownlike facility for bouncing back, sounding twice as eager to please. It was his strength, but it was also his weakness, robbing him of every shred of dignity and inviting a mixture of pity and contempt.

Diane's injury was not serious, but the Makaha contest was ruled out; ordered to keep her weight off the bruised and swollen ankle, she had the complete sympathy of the other surfers. She decided that it would be too painful to watch her feminine rivals carry off trophies that she was positive could have been hers. As a result, Diane was not among the spectators who watched Ron Tercotte and a disproportionate number of Linc's "team" distinguish themselves at the big international meet. Diane chose, instead, to sit on the porch of the Executive mansion, alternately brooding and cursing Eddy for her

109

misfortune. No one, except Laurie, bothered to remind her that she had been the victim of an accident and not a vicious conspiracy.

Diane's vindictive mood cast a pall over the safari's Christmas celebration; at least, she made the day a dismal one for Eddy, and, vicariously, for Laurie. Linc had planned an exchange of inexpensive gifts; each of the group's members was to buy one gift for someone whose name was pulled from a hat. Ironically, Eddy drew Diane's name and broke the rule about buying only token items.

Diane was presented with a costly sweater, which came with an ornate Christmas card on which was scrawled:

I'm sure sorry. I hope you win first next year.

Eddy.

Diane's only reaction had been a cool, "Thank you." Later, she was heard telling Goofyfoot that she wouldn't even bother entering next year unless "that creep" was banned from the Islands.

Furthermore, although Diane's disappointment was genuine and justified, she used her miserable plight for more personal advantages. Ron's natural sympathy for a promising champion who got cheated out of a chance to compete was milked dry.

"I know exactly how you felt," Ron assured her during the group's New Year's Eve party. "I couldn't have watched it, either, if I'd gotten cut out of competing." After which Laurie heard Diane ask Ron to give a wave-by-wave description of his successful heats in the contest. Their conversation closed out everyone else. Laurie spent the hours before midnight arguing with Linc, assuring Eddy that he was really an *excellent* dancer while avoiding his sandaled feet, and convincing Craig Barclay, who had been toasting the New Year with martinis since noon, that he was *not* an irresistible lover.

Miserable, Laurie was in bed by the time Ron helped Diane limp to the bedroom door. There was a whispered conversation, then a long lull before Ron said, "Can you manage the rest of the way?" and Diane murmured, "I think so, darling." A long, agonizing lull; Ron kissing Diane good night.

Typically inconsiderate, Diane flicked on an overhead light as she hobbled into the room, although Laurie had left a lamp lighted for her convenience.

Laurie winced at the sudden glare, although she had hoped to feign sleep.

Diane, who had come into the room dozens of times without a word of greeting, chose this occasion to be affable. "Oh — hi. I didn't know you were still awake."

"Just barely," Laurie told her. She resisted, as being too obviously jealous, an urge to turn her back on the sight of Diane examining her smeared lipstick in the dresser mirror. Diane was undeniably pleased by the effect. In the cool white linen-like shift she had chosen to show off her tawny skin, she looked too appealing for comfort, in spite of her bandaged ankle and bare feet. Laurie saw her for a moment through Ron's eyes, then closed her own.

"Neat party, wasn't it?" Diane persisted. "I had a fantastic time."

Is she reminding me that I didn't? Laurie wondered. The hazel-eyed sphinx couldn't have elected to break her silence just for a chummy girl-to-girl chat.

Diane wasn't interested in a response. "I noticed you had to keep old man Barclay at bay. He's made a couple of passes at me, but I told Ron he doesn't have to be jealous. When you let a wolf like that know you aren't interested, he'll leave you alone."

"I've *let* him know I'm not interested," Laurie said curtly.

"Maybe you weren't firm enough." Diane let the deliberate dig sputter in Laurie's consciousness while she pulled the white shift over her head and tossed it over a chair. With her casually cut dark hair disheveled, she managed an even more attractive gamin appearance. "How can his kid help being a moron, with a sickening specimen like that for a father?"

Laurie started to speak her mind in defense of Eddy, but Diane had gone to the bathroom and closed the door. A minute or two later, after much splashing and humming, she emerged, her face radiant without makeup, to pick up the conversational thread where she had chosen to cut it off.

"I was telling Ronnie tonight, old man Barclay tried getting next to me with a song and dance about how he didn't expect a girl surfer to be beautiful." Diane punctuated her remark with a sidelong glance into the mirror. The hazel eyes reflected satisfaction once again. "He expected me to look like some of those tough, muscle-bound bags he saw at Makaha."

"If you're talking about the girls who won first, second and third, and the girls who placed in the tandem," Laurie said, "I thought they were exceptionally attractive. Ron and Linc and I talked about it on the beach, as a matter of fact."

Diane fixed her usual fishy stare on Laurie. More accurately, she seemed to be staring *through* Laurie, without lowering herself to see her. "Oh? Really?"

"What's more, I talked to several of them between events. One in particular, because she's planning to be a nurse. And there was another pretty blond who's an airline hostess, I think. Darling girls — completely feminine, intelligent — good sports." Laurie tempered her criticism by smiling. "Maybe we're talking about different people."

It was plain that they weren't. Diane's face had twisted into a jealous mask that distorted her perfect features. "I didn't know you thought so much of my competition. You must have been thrilled to death when that idiot you're always praising put me out of the contest."

"That isn't true, Diane. I'd have been rooting for you, like everyone else in this group. I can't say I admire the way you've treated Eddy, considering that he was trying to do you a favor, and considering how awful he feels about what happened. But I'm sorry you didn't get to compete."

Diane released a disbelieving snort. "I can imagine. *Especially* since I had to quit surfing with Ron all day." She examined the mirrored reflection of her face more closely this time, rubbing at an imaginary lipstick smudge that hadn't been washed off. "I can sympathize. Ron dated you a few times and you got ideas about him. Most girls do." Diane whipped a brush through her hair, leaving the rest of her thought unsaid, but implying her message with a smug, confident stance: Most girls were crazy about Ron Tercotte; Ron was crazy about *her.*

"Is that what you wanted to get across?" Laurie asked.

The hazel eyes opened wider in an attempt at innocence. "I can't imagine what you're talking about."

Laurie settled back on her pillow and pulled the covering sheet over her shoulders. "You know, Diane, I have a confession to make. I was finding it uncomfortable, sharing a room with someone who was either too rude, too snobbish or too vapid to have anything to say to me. After hearing you tonight, I'll admit something else. I didn't know when I was well off."

Diane responded with a musical but mirthless laugh. "I'll *bet*," she said.

A long time later, she turned out the lights, lying in bed and whistling an irritating rock 'n roll tune between her teeth, undoubtedly to demonstrate that she was deliriously happy after a successful evening. It seemed that she would never fall asleep.

Laurie also lay awake, too proud to cry, too heartsick not to. Earlier, during the demeaning conversation with Diane, there had been boisterous sounds from the bigger house next door, where the New Year was still being welcomed by a few hardy souls. Over the tail-end-of-the-party noises there had been the jarringly shrill but familiar sounds of Craig and Vivian Barclay tormenting each other with another of their verbal wars. There had been only one refreshing note; Laurie had caught enough snatches of the argument to know that the battle was not exclusively concerned with Eddy; they were starting the New Year with vicious criticisms of each other's behavior at the party, and labeling each other with names that would have shocked a Port Said stevedore. Laurie had wondered how Eddy could go on listening to them, and still maintain his carefree facade. Had he armored himself against pain, or was there a lifetime of poison boiling inside him, waiting to erupt?

Finally those sounds had ceased, and now, except for the distant rush of the surf, the hours before daybreak were deathly still. In the silence, Laurie was flooded by a sense of strangeness. What was she doing here, in exotic surroundings, thrown together with people who were either separated from her by their interests, or downright hostile? She felt purposeless, her one justification for being here, her nursing ability, had become a farce; she had applied a gauze pad to the head of another stranger in this alien element.

She was rested now. Days of lolling on sunny beaches had brought fresh color to her cheeks; she had gained weight, and if she could escape the constant emotional pressures, her nerves would be steady again. In the eternally understaffed hospital back home, she would be needed again.

In a few days, now that Linc had accumulated more footage of Hawaiian surf than he could begin to splice into his film, the safari would be heading for Australia. What value would she have there, except as a tourist? No, not as a tourist; tourists have fun. They don't go out of their way to be tortured. Diane's triumphant entry into the room tonight . . . her pleased-with-herself smile . . . the smeared lipstick. . . .

Someone was padding around the house. Linc, getting ready for a pre-dawn excursion to check out another surfing spot?

Laurie listened intently, not because identifying the footsteps was of any great importance, but because any distraction from her morbid thoughts was welcome. She had determined that the night walker was too quiet to be Linc; his determined stride had a heavier sound.

Tiring of the guessing game, Laurie stopped craning her neck and turned over, hoping for sleep. It was then that she heard the crying sound — soft, jerking sobs that left no more question in her mind. It was Vivian Barclay.

Reason fought against instinct. Why get up and cause an embarrassing scene? Linc's advice: you can't help these people — they only drag you down. But suppose Eddy's mother was ill? What if she . . . ?

Laurie tossed the light covering aside, swung out of bed, and groped in the dark for her robe. Moving quietly, without turning on the light, she felt her way out of the bedroom, closing the door carefully behind her and tiptoeing past the room in which Eddy and Linc were sleeping.

Mrs. Barclay was still wearing the amethyst silk Chinese dress that she had bought especially for the New Year's Eve party. She was standing in the open doorway between the living room and the porch, leaning against the door frame in a disconsolate pose. In the pale light of approaching daybreak, Laurie noticed that although tears streaked the woman's face, they had not marred her carefully applied, waterproof mascara. Except for being in her stocking feet, she looked like a woman perfectly groomed for an important evening.

She seemed neither surprised nor abashed at Laurie's appearance. In spite of the hour, Laurie sensed that Vivian had almost *expected* someone to hear her, to wake up, and to come into the room.

Only the tritest, most obvious question sprang to Laurie's mind. "Is something wrong?"

"Everything," Vivian whispered. "Everything."

There was always a theatrical quality in Vivian's speech; as a showgirl, she had apparently dreamed of becoming an actress. But the whispered "everything," repeated after a well-timed dramatic pause, had in it the elements of pure ham. A brief resentment stirred inside Laurie. With emotional problems of her own, she was in no mood to pamper a woman who wanted to dramatize herself. Nor did she care to listen to a detailed recital of all the husbandly wrongs that constituted "everything."

Sorry she had left her room, Laurie offered a lame assurance, again falling back on a tired cliché. "Get some sleep. Things will look brighter in the morning."

It was, apparently, the perfect cue line for Vivian Barclay. "There . . . isn't going to *be* any morning." The sorrowful delivery of the line was as phony as that of a funeral director, but the cascade of tears that followed was genuine enough. Perhaps Vivian sounded artificial even when she meant what she said.

More irritated than shocked, Laurie asked, "What does that mean?"

Vivian walked out to the porch, staring out toward the sea. With that movie-finale bit of symbolism established, she said, "I don't want to live anymore! Eddy's growing up to be a . . . laughingstock. Craig may be dense enough not to know everyone's making fun of Eddy — yes, and playing Craig for a sucker, too. But I know it. And he's vile. Craig's vile! I watched him tonight — don't think I blame *you* — I watched him tonight, and I've watched him for years, chasing everything in skirts. How can Eddy have any respect for him? What kind of father image does he have?"

Vivian rambled on, her sentences jumbling together and becoming less coherent, until she was only sputtering, ". . . Hate him. Can't go on. Hate the sight of him!" She closed her eyes, swaying dizzily, holding on to the back of a chair for support.

It's too much, Laurie thought. An R.N. degree doesn't qualify or oblige me to play family counselor. (Linc's theory again: don't get involved, look out for yourself.) Still, every word the woman had said was true, and though her grief was embellished by degrading artifices, it was bona fide misery, nevertheless.

"Vivian — you aren't going to do anything that will hurt Eddy. He's been hurt enough. He needs you — both of you."

Vivian dissolved in a renewed outburst of tears, sobbing, "It's too late. I took pills . . . sleeping pills."

Laurie seized her shoulder. "How many? When?"

"Just now. The whole bottle. Fifteen. Twenty. I don't know." Vivian covered her face with her long, lacquer-tipped fingers, her body shaking convulsively. "It's too late — you can't save me."

There wasn't time to debate whether the woman was lying or telling the truth, whether this was an act of desperation or a faked bid for attention. Or to wonder, except fleetingly, why a despondent would-be suicide would dress to the hilt, sob loudly enough to be overheard, and immediately announce what she had done to the first person who responded. Laurie knocked on the door behind which Craig Barclay was sleeping, roused him, and then, although she loathed the risk of awakening Eddy, got Linc out of bed and explained the situation before tackling the job of administering emetics to Vivian.

Bedlam again. Craig surly and disbelieving one second, panic-stricken the next. Linc, barely awake, grumbling that he wished people would "hoke it up at more reasonable hours." And Vivian half hysterical, but genuinely frightened now, indicating that she had really gulped down the lethal dose, making a show of refusing to drink the antidotes Laurie prepared for her, but gulping them down desperately. The rising sun bathing the mountains with salmon-colored light as Linc raced them to a hospital in Honolulu, while Laurie devoted herself to keeping Vivian awake. All of it straight out of an incongruous nightmare. Especially Laurie's thought, faintly amusing even under the grim circumstances, of a woman laying on a thick coat of glamorous green eye shadow to go out and have her stomach pumped.

Nine

Laurie and Linc returned to the house at Sunset Beach shortly after ten that morning. Vivian Barclay had been pronounced out of danger, but she was considered far from emotionally stable. The hospital staff psychiatrist would be talking with her as soon as she was sufficiently recovered from the physical ordeal.

Craig Barclay had remained at the hospital (reluctantly, it seemed to Laurie), giving Linc the car keys and saying he would take a cab back "when this mess is over with." In Laurie's last view of him, the safari's "angel" was strolling a hospital corridor, puffing huge plumes of cigar smoke in the general direction of a NO SMOKING sign.

Since no note had been left for Eddy, and it had been impossible to reach him by phone, Linc took on the job of looking for him to break the news of Vivian's suicide attempt. Wearied by the sleepless night, Laurie tried napping. Diane, Ron, and the Barclays revolved in her brain like a dizzying kaleidoscope. There were glimpses, too, of the nurses at the hospital — pleasant, efficient, self-assured, with an obvious sense of belonging. It seemed years since she had worn a crisp white uniform and felt that she had a value to someone except herself.

Still sleepless, Laurie got up from her bed when she heard the screen door of the porch slam. It was after noon; she guessed that Linc had come to remind her that Gaston had lunch ready at the other house. She was surprised to see Craig Barclay in the living room. Looking somewhat disheveled in the sports clothes he had thrown on hastily before dawn, he apparently had added to his dissipated appearance by getting his cab to stop at a few Honolulu bars. He was mixing himself a drink as Laurie came into the room.

"I didn't expect you back so soon," Laurie said. "How is —"

"She's fine . . . groggy, but fine." Craig Barclay waved his free hand in a nonchalant gesture. "No reason for me to stay — I can't do anything for Vivian." Grudgingly he added, "Never *could*." And then, as though the subject was closed: "Fix one for you?"

"No, thanks. I . . . haven't had lunch."

"Give you an appetite," Craig persisted, holding the bottle of Scotch poised and ready for pouring a second drink.

Laurie shook her head. "No."

"Well, sit down and keep me company." Craig exhaled a self-pitying breath. "If you knew what that woman's put me through! This isn't the first time she's pulled this, you know." He carried his glass to a coffee table, indicating a seat on the sofa for Laurie, and settling himself close beside her.

Uncomfortable, Laurie regretted that she hadn't invented an excuse to leave the room. Being alone in the house with Craig Barclay, especially when he was drinking, was disconcerting enough. But having to listen to him berate a wife who was hospitalized. . . .

"Viv was in show business," Craig was saying. "She goes for these showy gestures. Doesn't care what happens to my nerves, not to mention the family reputation. Her people were trash — nobodies. Didn't have a dime. The Barclays have been established in California, all prominent people, since —"

"Mr. Barclay?"

His wispy mustache lifted over a sickeningly personal smile. "Craig," he insisted.

"Craig — I don't think this is the time to tear into Mrs. Barclay's background. She must have been miserable to do what she did. Maybe she's . . . theatrical. That's her nature. But she *could* have died. And . . ." Laurie weighed her next criticism briefly. ". . . I think it would help if you stayed with her as much as possible."

Craig sighed. "Honey. . . ." He punctuated the word by raising one hand and letting it drop, as though in a hopeless gesture, to Laurie's knees, ignoring her annoyed movement away from his touch. "Honey, you don't understand. I'm the last person on earth Viv wants to see when she flutters those phony eyelashes and opens her eyes." Craig edged closer to Laurie, and spoke in a low, confidential voice. "I don't want this to get around, but things aren't exactly lovey-dovey with the two of us."

If she hadn't been so apprehensive, Laurie would have laughed out loud. Anyone within a hundred yards of the Barclays, unless he was hard of hearing, didn't have to be let in on this "secret information."

"You see the way she treats me," Craig said between thirsty gulps from his glass.

"Ridicules me in public, makes scenes, tries turning my own boy against me. And then makes it look like I'm driving her to —"

Laurie started to get up. "Mr. Barclay, I'd rather not —"

The hand that closed around her shoulders was firmly persuasive. "Don't rush off, dear. You're a girl who understands men. What's your hurry?"

"I'd like to get up, if you don't mind." Inwardly, Laurie was seething, but she kept her voice politely cool.

"See, there you go! You're misunderstanding me, too. No reason to treat me like I'm Jack the Ripper, sweetheart. Any reason why we can't talk? Be friends?" Craig's unctuous tone, probably his idea of a sexy purr, was accompanied by warm, alcoholic fumes as he bent his head closer to Laurie's face. He was blocking her way deliberately now. "I could do a lot for a girl like you. Nice, understanding girl who —"

"*Will* you let me go?" Laurie demanded. She was struggling now to free herself from the unwelcome grip.

"Baby, what an *attitude!*" Craig protested. "Nobody's going to hurt you. You're on this trip for fun, aren't you? Well, then, let's not be so —"

Some time during Craig's oozing argument, the screen door had slammed.

"Let's not be so revolting, Craig."

Craig spun around at the sound of Linc Addison's voice. Laurie managed to brush Craig aside and get to her feet.

"I *think* Laurie was finding you revolting," Linc said. He was standing inside the doorway, looking completely relaxed, but Laurie noticed that his hands had tightened into white-knuckled fists.

Craig's face had turned a purplish red. Straining to appear casual, his voice betrayed him, and he sputtered, "Just . . . talking. No need to . . . play hero, Linc. The maiden's in no grave danger." His attempted laugh fell short of being believable.

Linc examined him as though he were vermin. "If you're in a talking mood, Eddy's coming in. I imagine you'll have a lot to say to him."

Eddy came charging across the porch a second later, out of breath and wide-eyed with concern. "Hey, Dad, I just heard about Mom. Is she okay now? Can we go see her? What's *wrong*, anyway?"

Linc nodded at Laurie, holding the screen door open for her. They were halfway across the lawn, on their way to the larger house, before Laurie said, "Nice

129

timing, thank you. It was getting sticky."

"With Craig, that's easily possible," Linc said.

"You got a little out of character, didn't you?" Laurie had relaxed enough to throw a wry smile in Linc's direction.

"You mean the shining-knight bit?"

"Uhuh. I didn't think you believed in getting involved. You could have turned around and let me fight it out with old itchy paws myself."

"I could have, yes," Linc agreed.

"You took quite a chance of losing your sponsor. He tried to act breezy, but you could tell he was furious."

"No risk," Linc said. "I have an iron-bound contract."

"Okay, *don't* let me make you feel like a two-fisted hero. All I know is, I was awfully glad to see you when you walked in."

Linc's cool pose melted and he grinned. "Flattery will get you everywhere with me." More seriously, he said, "Frankly, if I hadn't known Eddy was right behind me, I'd have had the fun of inflicting a semi-serious nosebleed. I've always thought that on Craig it would look good."

"I'm glad you restrained yourself," Laurie said. Somehow, she had picked up Linc's casual, facetious tone, perhaps because she realized that Linc was rejecting the virtuous hero-to-the-rescue role as embarrassingly square. "And I hope I haven't destroyed your image of yourself. You're still completely objective, indifferent, cool, removed."

"Certainly," Linc said. "My reason for wanting to belt Craig in the snoot was absolutely, unsentimentally selfish."

"Oh?"

"I was only looking out for Number One, as usual. Going on the theory that if anyone with frankly dishonorable intentions is going to make passes at you, it's going to be *me*."

He sounded perfectly sincere, leaving Laurie torn between a faint belief that he was bluffing, and the astounding but somehow more valid realization that Linc Addison meant exactly what he had said!

Vivian Barclay's suicide attempt was unknown to the surfers who had gathered for lunch around the long table. Yet Laurie doubted that any news which did not directly concern them or their sport would have dampened the mood of Toshi, Beast, Goofyfoot, or the others. Individually, they had made good showings at Makaha. They had been lucky in catching good surf at all the favorite winter spots, and Linc had recorded some fantastic rides on film. Now, packed and anxious to tackle Australian waves, their mood was irrepressible. Even Diane, whose ankle was nearly back to normal, was talkative and animated, and Ron's spirits had never seemed higher.

Over Gaston's Polynesian-style chicken and pineapple fritters, they were whooping it up about the next leg of their safari, when the talk turned to the Barclays.

"Hey, Linc, do we have to drag that trio of creeps with us to Sydney?" Goofyfoot wanted to know.

"If you want your bills paid, yes," Linc said. "Otherwise, no."

"Mo' beddah dey come alongside," Toshi decided, his pidgin more affected than usual.

Beast grunted something uncomplimentary about Eddy, and then commented on the fact that none of the Barclays was present at the table.

"Yeah, what'd they do?" Goofyfoot asked. "Crawl back under their rocks?"

"Bi-i-g e-motional problems," Diane said evenly. "They had a dilly of a fight last night."

"Are they still scrapping about that all-time wipeout — that ever-ready Eddy?"

Goofyfoot made a disgusted grimace. "They oughta trade him in on a new model."

"I don't know what it was all about," Diane said. "I *do* know they were keeping me awake. Laurie ought to know. She got up and got it settled and then they went for a ride. Anyway, I heard a car starting up."

"We went out to do a few night spots," Linc said.

Ron looked surprised. "You and Laurie double dated with the Barclays? Man, that's too much!"

"Must be some crazy night clubs around." Diane's comment had a caustic edge. "It was almost daylight when you left. I notice you're back, Laurie, and I saw *Mr.* Barclay pass by in a cab a while ago . . ."

"Okay, cool it," Linc ordered. "I don't dig this petty gossip jazz. Vivian's a little bent out of shape, so we drove her to the hospital." He got up, carrying his glass of milk with him. "I've got to check on those reservations. The airport's jammed with guys going back to the mainland, and I want to be sure our flight's bolted down for tomorrow."

Linc had assumed that the suicide attempt should be discreetly covered up, but his departure left Laurie to answer the

133

questions. The others would have forgotten the subject immediately, she was certain, but Diane seemed to be getting a perverse pleasure out of extending it.

"Where'd you go after you dropped off Mr. Barclay's wife, Laurie? You must have had a ball." Laurie ignored the taunting request for more information, but Diane persisted, addressing no one in particular. "Old Vivian was sobbing and putting on a big show. I had to put a pillow over my head to get to sleep."

"When I hear someone crying, I don't put a pillow over my head," Laurie said. She regretted the irritable outburst, especially since the words came out sounding sanctimonious. She mumbled the rest. "I try to help."

Goofyfoot had mounted his chair, launching into an imitation of a fire-and-brimstone evangelist. "Brethren an' sistren, I'm 'shamed of you! You got pillows over your heads. From now on, I say to you, take those pillows *off!*"

Someone yelled "Amen!" and everyone laughed, except Laurie.

"What you lack, brethren and sistren, is . . . you lack compassion. You take sister Laurie here. She's a do-gooder. A din-dandy do-de-do-do-gooder!"

134

"Yeah, man!" Toshi yelled out.

"Now, when Eddy takes off in front of you on your wave, are you gonna put dings in his head?"

"No!" Diane shrilled.

"No, brethren . . . and you, too, baby." Goofyfoot leaned down to wink at Diane. "You show *understanding*, hear? Man, you don't add to his trauma with *re*jection. You smother him with *love*."

Laurie squirmed in her chair, wishing she had left with Linc. Walking out now, with her dessert unfinished, would imply weakness on her part, and add to Diane's satisfaction. She toyed with her food, hoping that Goofyfoot would run out of wind.

He not only went on, but Toshi joined him, doing high-pitched, devastating imitations of Eddy, of the Barclays, and finally, of Laurie herself:

"Oh, I don't mind not having any fun. I *like* to listen to you, Eddy. Tell me again — how many flaphenstaphs does Switzerland export every year?"

"Sixty-three million."

"*Isn't that interesting?* Now tell me how you shot the curl on that four-inch wave in the Disneyland lagoon, Eddy." They went on and on, with Diane's hilarity far out of proportion to the humor. Finally Beast

135

yawned, abruptly announced that he was going to take a nap, and somehow, miraculously, everyone was leaving the table, and the painful burlesque ended as suddenly as though someone had clicked off a television set.

Laurie started for the Executive Mansion alone. Then, remembering that Craig and Eddy Barclay were there, she changed her course, walking instead toward the beach.

She didn't know how long she had been sitting and staring out at the sea, nursing her angry humiliation, before Ron came strolling across the sand. He was wearing Bermuda shorts topped by a LINC ADDISON FILM PRODUCTIONS T-shirt, and he wasn't carrying his board. His greeting implied that their meeting was accidental:

"Hi. I thought I'd grab one last look. Too bad it's closed out."

Laurie nodded. She was still too shaken by ridicule to feel friendly toward anyone who had participated in her torment. Ron, she had noticed, had found his friends' antics amusing.

"We were talking about looking around for some fun surf. We're all too bushed from the party to tangle with big waves," Ron was saying after a long silence. Then, as Laurie continued gazing out toward the horizon, he dropped down beside her. "Am I bugging you? I know you don't dig surf talk."

"It doesn't bug me," Laurie said. "But when it becomes the *only* topic people can talk about intelligently, it gets monotonous."

"So I'm boring you."

Laurie shrugged. "It's too bad. I used to find you extremely interesting when your interests were broader."

"Funny. I look out at Sunset and I can't seem to think of any fascinating conversational tidbits about surgery."

"Perfect," Laurie told him. "Snide, smug, sarcastic. You conform beautifully, Ron. You sound just like that pack of sadistic hyenas back at the house."

"So that's what you're all up tight about!"

Laurie pressed her lips together grimly, a pointed reply escaping her.

"That — horseplay! They weren't putting you down, Laurie. They —"

"*No.* They were putting themselves down."

"Hey, where's your sense of humor? Goof' and Toshi rib everybody — they make fun of themselves, half the time. They're all high about taking off for Australia, clowning it up. How can you get

137

all shook about a little kidding around?"

"I didn't mind them ridiculing me," Laurie said. "If being civil to a kid with Eddy's problems makes me a fool in their eyes — in *your* eyes, go ahead and have your big yocks."

"Then what . . . ?"

"It's the fact that they can't put themselves into Eddy's shoes that disgusts me. Compassion — that's a joke to them. It's corny; it's square to feel sorry for someone, to try easing the hurt a little."

"That's not true," Ron argued. "They don't dig maudlin sentiment, no. Neither do I. But if Eddy really needed a hand, every one of those guys would —"

"Would what? Save him from a burning ship? Cross Niagara on a tightrope wire to rescue him? What do you mean by 'if Eddy really needed a hand'? Some phony dramatic situation, where you and your buddies could do something heroic and boost your swollen egos a little more?"

"You're coming on awful strong, girl."

Laurie hurled a handful of sand down and got to her feet. "You're not an insensitive clod. You know Eddy's parents — what they expect of him, what they do to him. The more he tries, the harder he gets kicked. Does it ever occur to any of you

138

big, strong, brave heroes that Eddy has more guts than all of you put together? I've seen him after one of your hilarious hatchet jobs . . . after his folks get through with him, and you and all your callous friends cut him to ribbons. He's probably dying inside, but he comes back for more."

"Because he's not quite bright?" Ron ventured. He had risen to face Laurie. "Maybe because he asks for it?"

"You ought to take your crowd to a mental institution some day," Laurie cried. "If torturing misfits is your idea of fun, you'd have a barrel of laughs in a schizo ward."

"Oh, come off it, Laurie!"

She was crying now, trembling, and too carried away by the raking emotion to care how her words affected Ron. It was too late to care, anyway. "I don't expect much more from that pack of selfish surf bums. But I expected you to have a heart, Ron. You don't, though. You're as vicious and as shallow as the rest of them." Laurie caught a shuddering breath, her voice dropping to a near whisper. "What made me think you had what it takes to be a great doctor? A doctor has to care about people. He doesn't laugh when they're hurt, and he doesn't think it's square when someone else tries to help them." Dredging her mind for one final thrust, Laurie swiped at her tears with the back of her wrist. "I'm glad you're not going to be part of my profession! Tell *that* to Diane and the rest of your 'cool' crowd. That ought to make them howl!"

"Hey, wait a minute —"

She was running down the beach, sobbing like a lost child. Over. It was done with and over, but she hadn't really lost Ron because he had never belonged to her, and perhaps she had never even known him. Idolized him, idealized him, made him into an unrealistic golden image of the kind of man she could love. Yes, and loved him. *Still* loved him.

"Okay, run!" he was shouting. "Throw a lot of swill at me and run. Fine! Great! Groovy!"

He was shouting, but he wasn't running after her. She had made a fool of herself, made a dramatic scene that even Vivian Barclay couldn't have topped, all because of a dimwitted kid she would probably never see again. She was determined now to leave the safari and catch the next plane home. But there was a difference between being heartbroken and being sorry. You were only sorry when you hadn't spoken the truth.

Ten

Ordinarily, Linc would have accepted almost any news casually. Laurie's announced decision to leave the party shouldn't have rated more than a raised eyebrow and a toneless "Okay, later for you, honey." To Laurie's surprise, Linc reacted that night in a variety of ways, none of them indifferent.

Linc was disappointed. "We've just started to swing. Miss a chance to see Australia? You're out of your box, kid."

He was annoyed. "What a crumby trick. Where am I going to find another nurse between now and plane time tomorrow?" (He ignored the fact that taking a nurse along had been a last-minute whim engineered for Laurie's benefit. Or that nurses were available "down under.")

And Linc tried persuasion. "You can't leave me without a chaperone for Diane! Vivian's staying here at the hospital, y'know. I gathered she's talking about flying home next week to start divorce proceedings. She tried to get Eddy to go with her — told him he's a flop at surfing and why didn't he stop letting his old man make a sap out of him, but I guess Craig got to the kid first. Big pep talk about sticking with it and proving he's a man, etcetera. Anyway, what am I going to do with one chick in this crowd of guys?"

They were seated on the porch of the Executive Mansion, and Linc thumbed toward the house he had rented for his surf stars. Thumping electric guitars indicated a farewell party in progress, and if Diane was the only girl present, she certainly wasn't voicing any complaints.

"I'm sure Ron will protect her virtue," Laurie said pointedly. "She certainly doesn't need me to look after her."

"Can't make you change your mind, huh?" Linc sounded unbelievably wistful.

"No. I think they'll have better use for me at the hospital."

"It wouldn't help to tell you *I* wish you'd stay? Not for the ridiculous reasons I've just given you. Just because I like having you around?"

Laurie hesitated, and Linc applied his final technique. "Diane'll be delirious with joy."

"I'm sure she will."

"Yeah. Ron's been giving her a rough time all evening. Not just Diane specifically — he seems to be mad at the world. What did you say to him, anyway? Out on the beach? He came back here fuming."

A flicker of hope raced through Laurie. "He was angry?"

"You must have burned him, but good. So far tonight, the most heartwarming word anybody's gotten from him is 'get lost.' I think he's closed up in his room, taking his hostilities out on beer cans."

"Drinking?"

Linc laughed at the troubled response. "No. Smashing cans with one hand. You know . . . *ca-runch!* I do it myself when I'm bugged about something. Terrific therapy." Linc's right hand flexed in a powerful crushing motion. "Oh, well. Whatever you said to him, you got your point across. I imagine he's so furious with you, he'll be glad you aren't taking the plane with us tomorrow. Do you want me to get a reservation for you? For San Diego?"

Linc's face was a study in innocence, but his eyes anticipated Laurie's decision. "He was really upset by something I said?" Laurie asked.

"I wouldn't con you."

"And Diane would do flip-flops if I quit?"

"That's putting it mildly."

Laurie's eyes met Linc's for a long moment. "As a photographer, you'd make a good psychologist. You know that?"

" 'One of my lesser talents,' Mrs. Addison's boy said modestly. All right, Laurie. I consider the resignation withdrawn."

Laurie reached forward to squeeze his arm impulsively. "I hate you, Linc. You know so darned much about me, it's disgusting."

"Hate you, too," Linc said. "You're staying for the wrong reasons. I kind of hoped you wouldn't be able to tear yourself away from my company."

"That's a lot to ask," Laurie said. "Considering that you don't offer a girl anything more than a here-today-gone-tomorrow relationship. Girls are possessive creatures, Linc. You're so honest about your intentions, or your lack of intentions —"

"That no serious chick can afford to waste time on me?"

"That's a crude way to put it, Linc, but — yes. I suppose every girl has to see orange blossoms and a wedding veil somewhere off in the far, dim future. Otherwise, no matter how much she may admire a man . . . if she thinks there's absolutely no hope at all — if she knows positively that the man prizes his freedom more than anything else in the world —"

"Like I said. She can't waste her time." Linc's eyes were exploring Laurie's again, this time with an undefinable sadness. "It's a bad scene, isn't it? I like you, Laurie. I wish I could lie to you. Better still, I wish I was one of the guys who can make promises and permanent plans and all that sort of jazz. Because — take this for what it's worth — if I had it in me to make promises and keep them, I think I'd make them to you." He laughed suddenly, ruffling Laurie's hair. "You've really met some losers on this trip, haven't you? A proposition from a potbellied drugstore tycoon, a declaration of undying devotion from a goofed-up kid . . ."

"How did you know . . . ?"

"Eddy doesn't have any secrets. He told me you turned him down, but you were, quote, very nice about it, unquote. And now you've gotten pitched by a permanent bachelor. Forget it. Go on — get your clothes packed."

Laurie was searching for the words with which to tell Linc that she half-wished he hadn't declared himself unavailable; she wanted to tell him that she was fonder of him than of any man she had ever known. Except that there was a small matter of love to contend with. A small matter, in which her chances were exceedingly slim, but a matter so consuming that she was willing to follow the long odds halfway around the world in the feeble hope that Ron's anger meant something . . . promised something. . . .

Linc's countless talents apparently included clairvoyance. "Play it cool," he said. "Don't apologize to The Tercotte. Let him sweat a little. And, above all, don't give diplomatic recognition to the object of your jealousy. When you smile at Diane, make it a smile you could pour on a stack of hotcakes. You dig?"

"I dig," Laurie said. She was on her way to her room. "Aren't you going to join the party, Linc?"

"I think I'll stay here," he yawned. "Craig drove Eddy to the hospital. I believe the kid's going to spend the night there."

"So?"

"So I have some business details to discuss with Craig when he gets back."

It occurred to Laurie that Linc was staying in the house because he didn't relish the idea of leaving her alone with Craig Barclay, but it would have embarrassed Linc to be thanked for his protection. Laurie liked him enough to play it Linc's way. Coolly, casually, Linc-style, she called out, "Have fun."

"I always do," Linc said. For once, he didn't sound wholly convincing.

Eleven

"I dunno," Eddy sighed disconsolately. "It's not the same anymore."

A fifteen-hour flight lay behind them. Laurie had come down to the hotel dining room after a brief rest, to find Linc occupying a table with Craig and Eddy Barclay.

"Who'd want it to be the same?" Linc asked. "Sydney's a great city. You'll see miles of beaches, and you can just about name the kind of surf you want."

"That's not what I mean." It was the first time Laurie had seen Eddy show outward signs of the depression that she was certain plagued him even when he was chattering and smiling like a finalist in a personality contest. "I liked it better in the Islands."

"You just got here," Craig said sharply. "How can you find fault with a place . . ."

"It's not the place," Eddy said. "It's just . . ." He gestured at the impersonal

148

surroundings. "Staying in a big hotel, for one thing. At Sunset we had houses, and everybody was close together. Here, everybody goes his own way. We all used to eat together; we had some neat parties. I dunno. I can't get across the way I feel."

Craig Barclay shrugged and lit a fresh cigar. Linc finished his glass of milk and signaled to the waitress for another. Neither of them seemed interested in analyzing Eddy's disappointment.

It seemed clear enough to Laurie. The two houses at Sunset Beach had given a family-like atmosphere to the group. In spite of ridicule and rejection, Eddy had felt that he belonged to a team; he was part of something closely knit, intimate and exciting, and if his only value had been to run for ice cubes or to wax a board for one of his idols, he had, at least, felt a brief rapport with the others. Quartered in a hotel, sharing a room with his father now that Vivian Barclay was absent, Eddy probably had the not-unfounded suspicion that the others might take off on predawn searches for good surf without bothering to call him.

In addition, the safari had dwindled considerably; a number of Linc's stars had remained in Hawaii to take advantage of the less crowded waves now that the Makaha contest and holiday crowds had gone back to California. "It's just not the same," Eddy repeated.

It was the story of his life, Laurie thought. His home life, his one-sided friendships, his inevitable blunders and his school failures, had all contributed to Eddy's sense of instability. He looked back upon every short-lived human contact with nostalgia.

Craig had suddenly decided to acknowledge his son's presence. "I'd say this is a great opportunity for you, Ed. The competition was heavy back in Hawaii, so you . . . held back. Maybe it wasn't your kind of surf. You heard what Linc said, son. You'll find exactly what you want here, and you can tear the place apart."

Linc gave his sponsor a weary glance, without going into detail about the formidable competition in Australia, and without mentioning that Eddy wouldn't have offered much challenge to the average beginner.

"That's what I'm hoping you'll do," Craig went on. "You don't have your mother here, cramping your style, telling you to be careful, or constantly pounding it into your head that you aren't good

150

enough and that big surf is too dangerous. Well, now you're among *men*, Ed. You've got a chance to justify this big expense I've taken on." Craig fixed a challenging gaze on Eddy's bewildered face. "I gambled on you, son. I'm counting on you to prove you've got what it takes."

Meaningless, empty, phony-male phrases — the ridiculous "challenges to manhood" that frustrated windbags like Craig had been mouthing since time immemorial, and which had caused fools like Eddy to throw their lives away on precipices, in duels, in caves, and in wars. The only valid challenge had to come from within, and it had to be followed by irresistible but reasoned action. Unlike Ron and Linc, Eddy had not been dared to ride a monstrous wave by the wave itself. He was being egged on by a father whose own flagging ego needed a vicarious boost.

Laurie glanced at Linc, inviting him to straighten out Craig Barclay's thinking. But since the incident at the Executive Mansion, relations between the two men had been somewhat strained; Linc only maintained communications when expenses were involved. Now, he said nothing to contradict Craig — nothing to warn Eddy.

Craig finished out the lesson by lauding a young Aussie he'd read about who, in 1961, had been the first surfer to conquer the ferocious bombora, an outside break off Queenscliff, north of Sydney. He had, understandably in this sports-loving country, gained the status of a national hero as a result. "That's the kind of stunt that puts you up at the top," Craig said, directing his words at Eddy with the subtlety of a barbed lance. "The boy was only twenty-one at the time."

Linc excused himself and got up from the table, letting his expression speak for him.

Eddy seemed brighter now, or perhaps he was only anxious to end his father's taunting description of someone else's victory. He asked about plans for the next day in his more customary eager-beaver tone.

"I'm going to cover some of the beaches with Ron and Toshi and a couple of the outstanding locals," Linc said. He rattled off a list of places with intriguing names — Voodoo Bay, North Narrabeen, Bellambi, Dee Why and North Curl Curl. Yes, Eddy could tag along if he wanted to, though they were being chauffeured in a local surfer's car and board space was limited.

The invitation wasn't extended to Craig

Barclay or to Laurie, and Laurie learned the next day that Diane hadn't been included in the party, either. Linc's movies were not collections of haphazard shots; his films followed a theme and told a story, and apparently his plans for the first day revolved around his two best big-wave riders and several Sydney-area stars.

To avoid both Craig Barclay and Diane, Laurie left the hotel alone and spent most of her first full day in booming Sydney sightseeing. The day only pointed up her ludicrous position; what sense did it make to have a nurse along as part of the safari, when she was left behind to shop and visit points of interest, like an ordinary tourist? Accepting a salary for doing nothing, from a man she had learned to detest, added to her rancor.

Eddy had been right; nothing was the same. There wasn't even the hope of seeing Ron at mealtimes now, and, in any event, Ron was doing a good job of pretending that Laurie didn't exist.

She returned to the hotel shortly after four in the afternoon. Surprisingly, Linc, Ron, Toshi, Beast, and Diane were gathered around a small table on the hotel terrace sipping soft drinks. Linc hailed Laurie, and Toshi reached out with his foot to pull a chair over for her.

"I didn't expect you back this early," Laurie said.

"We didn't expect to *be* back this early," Toshi echoed.

The group exchanged dark, knowing glances, and it didn't take much questioning to discover why.

"We've been here since noon," Linc said. "Why didn't I belt Craig in the mouth last night when he got started on that bombora tale? It was like telling the kid, 'Go out and be a hero, or else.' And I didn't shut him up!"

Laurie drew in a quick breath. "Eddy."

"Yeah, Eddy," Ron sighed. "Tell me why you had to drag him along, Linc? Give me one reason why you don't ship him back home?"

"Because we need the Barclay bread," Linc reminded him. "You cats want to go to Peru for the contest in February, don't you? Okay. Eddy stays. It's in the contract."

"Maybe his old man will start getting the bit after today and pull out," Toshi suggested.

"I said there's a contract," Linc snapped.

"Will someone please tell me what happened?" Laurie pleaded.

"We're at Fairy Bower," Toshi said. "The

Bower, for your edification breaks fast over a big rock —"

"Skip the history," Ron ordered. "She doesn't dig all the technical terms."

Diane laughed, and Toshi continued, "Anyway, we looked the Bower over and it was a mess. Ten-, twelve-foot waves whomping over, closing out on the wrong swell, too lined up, starting to blow out, tide was wrong —"

"Unrideable," Diane summed up. She addressed Laurie condescendingly, as though she were talking to a retarded toddler.

"We didn't even take our boards off the car rack," Toshi continued. "We're just standing around talking to some of the locals for a while, and then Linc says let's split and see if it's any better down the line. And that's when we hear all this yelling and whistle blowing. *Man!*" The little sun-blackened surfer slapped his forehead with his hand. "The first thing I see is Eddy's board. He must have taken it off the rack when we weren't looking. You tell her, Linc. I can't even describe it."

"Well, the kid evidently paddled out and made it through the shorebreak," Linc said. "Don't ask me how. I guess he got caught in a sneaker set —."

155

"A row of unexpected waves," Diane said, using her kindergarten-teacher intonation.

"I don't know what happened — maybe he got sucked over the falls. By the time we knew what was happening, we couldn't even see Eddy. We just saw his board smashing into pieces on the rocks."

A wave of horror shuddered down Laurie's spine. If Eddy hadn't made it, would these "cool" characters be sitting here, disgusted because their safari had been spoiled? "What about *Eddy?*"

She was wrong, and Laurie regretted the unfair thought in the next instant. "We were sick," Linc said. "Just that board slamming around in the wild water. No sign of the kid." He shook his head. "They've got the world's most fantastic lifeguard crews down here. There were three official guards paddling out in a matter of seconds. Not only that, but before any of our guys could move, about four or five local surfers were out there —"

"And that took *hair,*" Toshi interrupted. "The kid's crazy, but these guys *knew* what they were getting into."

"And about six million years later," Linc concluded, "we see one of the guards coming back in with our hero on his board.

156

Danm fool kid didn't even need artificial respiration. He just flopped on the beach like a sick porpoise. All the odds said he should have been drowned."

Laurie felt air returning to her lungs. "Is he all right now?"

"Up in his room," Ron said.

"What makes him tick?" Toshi asked. "Somebody please tell me what would make him do a thing like that?"

Before either Linc or Laurie could explain why Eddy had decided to ride an unrideable surf, Diane added a comment that cemented any doubts Laurie had entertained about her character. "You must have felt like two cents," she said. "I mean, here we are, the big champs from California, and that stupid wipeout has to get himself rescued by Australian lifeguards. Makes us all look cheap."

There was a momentary silence, during which everyone turned to stare at Diane. Everyone, including Ron. Perhaps she realized the callousness of her evaluation, because she added quickly, "It's good they hauled him in, but it sure put the rest of us down. You know what I mean."

Linc only glared at her. The others looked somewhat startled, although they had obviously been irritated by Eddy's stu-

157

pidity. In Toshi's dark eyes and on the usually expressionless face of Beast there was now an unmistakable hostility, and it was Ron Tercotte who said at last, "We know what you mean, Diane. We just didn't happen to be thinking of our reputations at the time."

It was a sentence that stayed with Laurie for the rest of the day; a hopeful message that made it easier to console Eddy and to ask the others to treat him, when he was able to emerge from his room and face them, as though nothing had happened.

Twelve

Ron, Beast, and Toshi had made it clear that the near loss of a human life could not be equated with their "image" in Aussie eyes. Furthermore, to Laurie's relief (and certainly to Eddy Barclay's), the debacle at the Bower was passed over as though it had never happened. But their attitude toward Eddy had in no way changed. In their eyes, he was still a clod, and he was brushed off accordingly.

Several days after Eddy's ill-fated attempt to "prove himself," all eight of the remaining safari members were ending the afternoon at a gently sloping, unpatrolled beach. Giant pine trees edged the road behind them, and the surf they faced was almost negligible. They had been cruising the coast all day, finding no waves that deserved to be recorded by Linc's camera. Tired of the search, they had decided to rest on the inviting sands before returning

159

to the hotel. Eddy had "helpfully" un-loaded all the boards before Linc could stop him, but only Toshi had paddled out into the unpromising waves.

"Old Tosh' never gets enough," Linc commented. "He'd surf in a fishbowl if he couldn't find anything better."

"Look at him sitting out there." Ron laughed. "Looking over his shoulder like he's hoping something will materialize."

As a gag, Ron and Beast ran to the water's edge, waving their arms and yelling, *"Outside! Outside!,"* the surfers' in-dication that a set of waves is forming be-hind them.

"Down here, they holler 'Out the back,' " Linc corrected.

If Toshi heard the others, he ignored them, bobbing on his board with patient calm. Ron stretched out in the sand and Beast soon joined him.

"Tomorrow we'll caravan up the coast and have a look at Crescent Head and Angourie," Linc said. "Maybe it'll improve back here while we're gone."

An indolent, rather demoralized mood had fallen over the group. Craig Barclay mumbled something about expenses going on, with no film being exposed. Linc re-minded him sharply that you couldn't control waves the way you controlled a drugstore inventory, and Diane wondered aloud why they had to sit around wasting time "just so Toshi can improve his tan."

"We can always swim," Laurie suggested. The water looked tempting — especially since most of the other spots they had visited were surfing beaches, closed to swimmers.

Diane tossed her a contemptuous glance. "Swim? Swim? Oh, sure. That's what you do when you get wiped off your board."

Everyone was quiet. Eddy decided it was time to liven up the atmosphere with some of his carefully memorized "conversation starters." Apropos of nothing at all, he piped, "Hey, I read something interesting that I'll let you guys try to figure out. Sort of a guessing thing."

Beast groaned. *"Why?"*

"Well, we're just killing time, so this'll be interesting. Dad, this is right up your alley. There was this druggist in Lansing, Michigan, see. He was in business for sixty-one years, and then he retired at the age of eighty-one."

"Fascinating," Ron said.

Craig scowled at his son. "Ed, I don't think anybody cares about —"

"No, this is really *interesting*," Eddy argued, "I made a . . . kind of a brain-teaser out of it." No one turned or paid the faintest bit of attention to him, but he plodded ahead cheerfully, looking to Laurie for encouragement. "The question is, how many prescriptions would you say this guy filled in his whole career?"

"Nine," Beast growled.

"Like, who cares?" Diane asked.

"Guess," Eddy urged. He couldn't have been completely oblivious to the cold reception his "guessing game" was receiving, but he had gone this far and apparently he was anxious to reveal his specialized knowledge. "How many would you say, Laurie?"

"Oh . . . ninety thousand," Laurie guessed.

"Wrong. How 'bout you, Ron?"

"I'm fast asleep," Ron said.

"Why don't you wise up, Wipeout?" Diane cried out. "Hasn't anyone ever told you you bug people?"

Laurie found it awkward to come to the rescue. "He's just making conversation."

"Boring conversation," Craig Barclay said. The contempt in his voice was as scathing as Diane's.

Eddy blushed, disturbed now. He made a stab at self-ridicule. "Yeah, I guess nobody cares that it was three hundred thousand."

Ron slapped his bare thigh. "That tears it! You can't shut this clown up."

"Get on your board," Beast suggested. "Go on, Eddy. Paddle out and tell Toshi how many sardines Nova Scotia packed in 1907."

"I was sort of thinking I might go out," Eddy stammered. He looked as close to tears as Laurie had ever seen him.

"Great idea," Diane said. "Give us a nose-riding demonstration, Champ. Toes over the nose. Show us how to hang ten."

Craig Barclay ground his cigar out in the sand. "That's what you get for talking like an idiot." He hurled the words at Eddy angrily. "How many times have I told you to start acting your age? You bore people. You embarrass me. You're a flop at everything! And look what it's cost me, just to give these leeches a few laughs." He got to his feet, livid with rage, and started toward the parked cars. Then, evidently changing his mind, he said, "A man wants to be proud of his kid. I'm about ready to give up on you. Let your mother take over — I've had it!"

Eddy wasn't listening. His own board had been smashed beyond repair, and now

163

he picked up Linc's, asking sheepishly: "Okay if I borrow your board, Linc? I won't ride it, or anything. I just want to paddle out."

Linc waved his consent.

Diane added a final barb. "Don't turn on the way you usually do. Toshi gets jealous when you show him up." She laughed, then resumed her sunbathing pose.

The others were quiet, perhaps even embarrassed by the cruelty of Craig Barclay's tirade. Only Laurie watched as Eddy pushed Linc's board into the water, mounted it after a clumsy struggle, and, kneeling, started paddling out toward the placid water beyond the mild surf. He had pointed the board to a place yards away from where Toshi Nomura sat like a waiting decoy. Eddy had finally "gotten the bit"; he didn't belong with others.

When he reached the glassy water, Eddy straddled the board, looking out toward the sea. To Laurie, his dejected form, silhouetted against the blue horizon, looked like a distillation of all the loneliness in the world.

She didn't remember consciously deciding to tell the others what she thought of them. It was as though an accumulation of resentments had reached the point of explosion inside her, and suddenly she was standing up and shouting, "Are you satisfied? All of you — are you proud of yourselves?"

They were staring at Laurie as though she had gone mad, and Linc managed to say, "Maybe we were a little rough, but he'll get over it."

"He's *been* getting over it," Laurie cried. "Time after time, he's been hurt and he's come back to let you hurt him again. What gives you that right? Just because you can balance yourselves on a piece of fiber glass you think you're *gods*. It's a cinch you aren't human beings! You're too vicious to —"

"Cool it, will you?" Diane muttered. "Hysterics bore me. We put down a kook and you have to throw a big scene —"

"Now, wait a minute!" Craig Barclay had turned his wrath on Diane. "I've had enough insults from you, young lady. If it wasn't for my son, you wouldn't be here on my money. You —"

"Your son!" Laurie spun around to face Eddy's father. "If he's been insulted and ridiculed, you've got yourself to blame. You've subjected him to every kind of humiliation — you've cut him to pieces your-

165

self. Why? To bolster your own ego? To get back at your wife? Well, you can't *buy* success for Eddy. You've only tortured him, trying to make him over into something you wish you were." Laurie waved her arm, indicating the startled group around her. "Trying to make him as cold and selfish and dehumanized as this — this pack of phony heroes. You sicken me! The lot of you!"

Linc had gotten to his feet, reaching out toward Laurie with a pacifying gesture. "Okay, you made your point. Now let's —"

"You, too!" Laurie had given up trying to hold back her tears. "You're the one who knows what Eddy's up against. You're the one who's used him to get what you want. And he worships you! *He calls you his best friend!*"

"Laurie, listen . . ."

She was sobbing wildly, running away from the group on the beach, knowing that she hadn't made any dents in the icy armor they wore, and not even feeling relieved by having cried out what she thought of them.

Without thinking, she raced toward the ocean, splashed through the shallow edge and finally dove through the first small wave that rolled toward her. Chilled by the sudden contrast in temperature, she shivered, stood for a moment in the waist-high water, and then started swimming toward the spot where Eddy Barclay was keeping a lonely unhappy vigil.

Cutting through the water with a strong, steady crawl, Laurie's body felt refreshed and her mind had started functioning clearly once again. She would swim out, chat with Eddy for a while, then go back to the hotel and pack her suitcases. Linc's philosophies were not for her, and Ron was a lost cause. Her only function on this trip had been to patch the battered morale of a misfit kid. Now, for the last time, if she couldn't cheer him up, she would at least have company for her own misery. In this crowd, she and Eddy Barclay had a lot in common.

Eddy evidently didn't see her swimming toward him. And, perhaps still hopeful that *someone* would welcome his presence, as Laurie approached he abruptly started paddling toward the lineup where Toshi waited for a rideable wave. Laurie changed her course, intending to meet Eddy at his new destination. She took several long strokes, then treaded water, looking out to pinpoint her direction. Toshi saw her and waved, flashing his quick grin and yelling, "How you stay, Seestah?"

The grin was so infectious that it was hard to remember that Toshi had been excluded from her angry accusations only because he hadn't been on the beach a few moments ago.

"Come 'longside, dees fella show you da kine way you ride," Toshi shouted over the hushed noise of the surf. In the next instant, he flicked an intuitive glance over his shoulder. A rising mound of water forming behind him evidently held the promise he had been waiting for. Lying prone on his board, he made a single long stroke with his arm and rose to his feet with the catlike agility that had earned him his reputation in the surfing world.

Laurie's eyes opened wide in amazement. Out of an almost glassy sea the swell had towered to an imposing height, and Toshi let out a triumphant yell. He was driving left, completely locked in the wave, delirious with his unexpected good luck. Well out of his path, Laurie froze, hearing the rider's joyous cry turn into a warning shriek.

Toshi must have seen the board and the floundering, bewildered figure before Laurie did, but locked into a position where he had no maneuverability, there was no way to avoid the specter that had materialized before him. There was only Toshi's savage curse, Eddy's cry of alarm, and the crunch of fiber glass as Toshi's speeding board shot into the obstacle. Then the wave poured over, obscuring Laurie's view, turning her over in a series of uncontrollable somersaults before she emerged, sputtering, to survey the results of the crash.

Linc's board, probably badly damaged, was flopping toward the beach. Toshi, further out, was swimming to retrieve his. And Eddy, with his gift for unexpected appearances, was at Laurie's side, paddling the water like a drowning pup and gasping, "Oh, man, I've had it! Linc'll kill me. Tosh'll kill me first."

"You aren't — hurt?" Laurie puffed.

"No. I just — wish I was — dead."

"Toshi — seems to be okay," Laurie said. "We'd better get — back in. That was a — weird thing — that wave. Might be more."

"I got psyched." Eddy too was having trouble getting his breath. "I got paralyzed; it — came up so fast. Man, all the guys were watchin' —"

He was right. As Laurie turned to swim back toward the beach, she saw Linc, Ron, and the formidable hulk of Beast lined up at the water's edge. They had been joined by two local surfers, and all of them had undoubtedly seen the collision. To Eddy, they must have looked like an angry mob, waiting to pounce on him. Linc had started wading out to rescue his new custom-shaped board from further damage on the rocky strip of beach toward which it was being tumbled.

Was Toshi responsible, for not making sure his way was clear before taking off? The protocol was beyond Laurie's knowledge, but the rules wouldn't matter. Without Eddy, it wouldn't have happened; his guilt was determined. And Eddy's dread of facing the group on the beach was a palpable thing that transferred itself to Laurie.

She had taken only a few strokes shoreward when a piercing cry from the beach stopped her. Looking toward the sand, she saw one of the Australians pointing frantically toward the water. *"A Dean! A Dean!"*

The warning shout assaulted her ears in almost the same second that her mind registered Ron's scream: *"Laurie! Swim for shore! Hurry!"*

She had a flashing glimpse of Ron and the others racing for their boards. Heart pounding, she started to obey the terrified order, when another chilling cry stabbed her consciousness. It came from Toshi, only a few yards behind her, and in the instant that she turned her head in his direction, she remembered what the Australians meant by "a Dean." Her memory was jogged by a frightening reminder; as Toshi screamed again, one arm grasping desperately for the board beyond his reach, an awesome gray fin cut the surface of the water beside him.

For an instant, Laurie was motionless with horror. Then plunging forward, propelled by fear, she looked around for Eddy.

It had to be a nightmare! Eddy wasn't swimming toward the beach. Flailing his arms and legs in insane splashing motions, he was making his way back toward Toshi. Someone on the shore was shrilling, "He's going the wrong way! Eddy! My God, Eddy!"

"Eddy!" The echo was Laurie's own voice, but the wildly kicking figure was threshing its way to where Toshi's cries filled the air, and a second curved fin had added its menace to the first.

Nightmare. Damned fool kid, doing the wrong thing, going the wrong way. All his life a series of stupid blunders, and now. . . .

Like someone drowning, Laurie recalled

darting conversations: Eddy's "statistics" about sharks; Eddy revealing a fact that "most people didn't know" — that sharks could be frightened off by churning and splashing the water near them — a discredited "fact" that Linc and Ron and the experienced Aussie surfers had ridiculed. But Eddy had read it in an old Navy manual. True or not, it might give Toshi a chance.

True or not, *two* people coming to Toshi's aid would improve the odds. A nurse's life was devoted to saving lives. *Two* sharks. *Two* people swimming the wrong way, stirring up the water, beating it into a froth with their arms and legs. *"Most people don't know this, but it's a very interesting fact. . . ."*

Suddenly the nightmare under the sun became a series of blinding, deafening, soul-searing impressions: Eddy's stricken cry, and a swirl of pink water where he had been splashing. A fin, and a long, dark shadow under the water; a rapacious, eight-foot-long shadow, confidently unmindful, in its hunger, of Laurie's hysterical slapping bout with the sea.

Laurie had a momentary thought: *it can't last long, and then it will be over.* Then the sound of anxious voices, the sight of boards racing toward her like bullets.

"Get the kid, Beast!"

"Over here, mate!"

"You blokes see to *her.*"

She was fainting, and a pair of strong brown arms grasped her body, and pulled her up to the cold, hard surface of a surfboard. Someone was crouched over her, breathing hard, paddling the board toward the sand with sure, powerful strokes. And the voice that sounded strangely like a man crying, was Ron Tercotte's voice, saying over and over again, "Oh, my God, Laurie — you're all right, you're all right — you're safe, you're all right! *Laurie, Laurie — Laurie!*"

Thirteen

She had not fainted, and once her feet had touched the sand, Laurie could not afford the luxury of hysteria or tears. The boards that followed Ron's carried two badly mangled forms, either dead or, considering their condition, blissfully unconscious. There were other hysterical responses to the carnage; Laurie steeled herself to ignore them.

Yet the horrified reactions from people who had never forced themselves to remain efficiently calm in a hospital emergency room were understandable. Toshi's left arm, almost severed near the elbow, lay at a grotesque angle across his chest. He was bleeding only slightly less profusely from numerous abrasions made by the coarse sandpaper-like swipes of sharkskin. Eddy's thigh had been severely mauled, and another crescent-shaped bite on his left leg was draining his life blood.

Laurie had no time to be stunned by the gruesome sight. Seconds after the boys had been dragged to the sand, the boards serving as stretchers, she was tearing someone's sport shirt into strips. Ron was at her side, neither of them saying a word to the other, yet each instinctively knowing where to tie the tourniquets first, working together with the desperate but calm coordination that exists in operating rooms and nowhere else — between doctors and nurses, and no one else.

While he worked, after determining that neither of the patients needed artificial respiration, Ron took charge, barking crisp, authoritative commands:

"Beast — get those blankets from the car! And the ice chest. Hustle!"

"Blankets and *ice?"*

"Don't argue — they're in shock *now!* Mike — how far are we from a telephone?"

"Dave's already driven off to call an ambulance," someone with an Aussie accent replied. "But we're twenty minutes from the nearest phone."

Ron calculated the time before help could be reached; the ambulance trips to the remote beach and back to the city. "Too long to wait," he decided. "We'll drive them to Sydney. Stay with us, will

175

you, fella? We'll need a guide to the nearest hospital."

"Count on it, mate."

Laurie tightened the tourniquet above Eddy's more severe leg wound. Strangely, she looked to Ron for her next move, and came close to addressing him as "Doctor."

Beast had come running with two blankets over his arm and lugging the portable cooler in which soft drinks had been carried to the beach.

"Watch the sand!" Ron barked. "Here, Laurie — get the kid covered. You fellows carry him to the station wagon." He was addressing Beast and the local boy he'd called Mike. "Craig, walk alongside — don't let him roll off the board. Leave room for Toshi. Linc'll help me carry him over in a second."

Craig Barclay, who had been too stunned to say anything until then, walked beside his son as the others carried him toward the parked cars. "What'll I tell Vivian?" he kept repeating. "How am I going to face Vivian?"

Only Linc and Diane remained as spectators. Until then, Laurie had been too busy to pay attention to their reactions. Now, suddenly, she could hear nothing else. Linc, who had kept up an anguished, completely out-of-control outpouring of questions and recriminations, was still blaming himself and asking, "Is he going to live? What are you doing? God, why did I let anybody go out where they haven't laid down shark nets? Ron, tell me — are you sure you know what you're doing?" And, then, "He's so white! All that blood! Laurie, can't you do something more? He's dead, isn't he? Toshi's dead!"

Among Linc's myriad talents, a gift for reasoned, unemotional efficiency in a medical crisis was not included. He was horrified, and he was helpless now. The confident self-assurance that was Linc's hallmark had been swept away.

"Will you shut up, Linc? Just stand back and be quiet?" Ron was digging into the insulated chest for crushed ice, a maneuver that puzzled Laurie and seemed to be causing an unnecessary delay. "Tell *her* to shut up, too."

Ron was referring to Diane. Linc had obeyed the order to be quiet, but Diane Etheridge hadn't stopped making hysterical noises since the boys had been carried from the water. Why she hadn't fled from the terrible sight was anyone's guess, her only contribution thus far had been an unnerving series of cries that she couldn't stand it — it was too ghastly and she couldn't stand it.

"Why don't you go and sit in the car?" Laurie told her now. "You aren't helping any."

"What's he *doing?*" Diane shrieked. "Toshi's arm! Oh, his *arm!* What's Ron *doing* to him?"

Ron was packing the nearly severed limb in ice, his own hands suddenly shaky, though he had maintained a professional calm thus far. It was obvious that Diane's hysteria was affecting his nerve, and nerve was all he had to sustain him. "Watch the *sand,*" he cried. "Get away from here, Diane. Out of my light."

Was it morbid fascination or had the shock of seeing two mangled bodies thrown Diane's judgment off balance? Instead of running, she pressed closer, the sand that clung to her bathing suit posing a threat to Toshi's open wounds as she leaned over him. "You'll kill him, Ron! His arm's almost torn off! What are you doing to him?"

"Get her out of my way!" Ron was securing the ice pack with an impromptu dressing torn from his T-shirt. Linc had turned his back on the scene. His face blanched, his legs trembling, he looked as

though he might be sick. Certainly he wasn't in any shape to get Diane under control. Ron was completing his strange operation and Laurie was crouched nearby, ready to cover Toshi with the second blanket. As Diane's hysteria mounted, Ron murmured, "I can't, Laurie. *You* do it."

Clutching the blanket in one hand, Laurie shot up to her feet from the crouching position, her free hand locked in a tight ball. The thudding impact of her fist against Diane's chin put an abrupt end to the nervewracking sound. A quick shove toppled Diane to the sand, well out of Ron's way.

Diane was still lying there, conscious, but whimpering, when the Australian boy came back to help Ron and Linc carry Toshi to the station wagon.

Fourteen

Some of Linc's feeling of helplessness came over Laurie during the long vigil at the hospital in Sydney. While teams of doctors and nurses fought to keep Toshi Nomura and Eddy Barclay alive, there was nothing for her to do but pace the corridors and pray, or to sit in the hospital reception room with the others, waiting in unbearable suspense.

There were four of them — the same four who had accompanied the boys on the wild ride to the city. Craig Barclay appeared on the verge of nervous collapse. Linc was silent in his dejection; he had surfed with Toshi for more than five years, and he couldn't help remembering Eddy's devotion to him. No one could suggest, now, that he was cool and detached.

And Ron? Since his almost prayerful gratitude that Laurie had escaped the ordeal unharmed, and since their frantic efforts on the beach, he had lapsed into a brooding silence of his own. Like everyone else, he was shocked and he was worried. But, it seemed to Laurie, he was thinking of something else, too — locked in a deeply personal, inner argument with himself.

At about ten-thirty that night, Linc broke into the tense silence. "They're doing all they can, Craig. They tell me they have an adequate supply of blood for transfusions. Why don't you let me drive you back to the hotel?"

"I'd get some sedatives from one of the doctors first," Ron advised. "Linc's right, Mr. Barclay. You can't do any good here."

Craig shook his head. "I can't leave."

"Sure you can," Linc urged. "You got your call through to Vivian. She'll be here in the morning and you'll be exhausted."

Craig looked around the reception room absently, his eyes swollen and red. "I feel like I'm going to keel over. Why don't they *tell* us something?"

"Eddy's holding his own," Ron said. "He's under heavy sedation. Toshi's going to be in surgery for hours. All you can do now is wait, and you'll be in better shape to . . . get your wife through the shock if you get some rest."

Another half hour dragged by before

Eddy's father reluctantly let himself be talked into leaving the hospital. He looked bedraggled and ludicrously out of place in his beach clothes; they all did. As Linc steered him to the door, Craig stopped in front of Laurie's chair, his voice a sheepish croak. "Why should you stay? You've already done enough for Eddy."

Ron answered for her. "We have a . . . professional interest, too, Mr. Barclay. Don't worry. We'll call you if there's anything to report."

Craig nodded dumbly. "I care, you know. He's my boy. Maybe I haven't done the right things for him, but —"

Laurie felt an overwhelming pity for the man — for his torment and for his aching conscience. "I'm sorry about the things I said," she told him gently. "I know you love him."

"They were true," Craig muttered. "Everything you said — it was all true." He blinked back incipient tears and made a weak show of bravado, relighting a tattered cigar. "It's sad, isn't it? The one time I'm really proud of Eddy — even though he made a mistake, he still showed more courage than I ever dreamed he had — the one time I want to tell him he's made me proud I'm his father, I — can't tell him."

"You will," Linc said. But the assurance was a hollow platitude. No one could promise that Eddy would live to hear Craig Barclay's first words of praise.

For a long while after Craig and Linc had gone, Ron sat staring at his hands, saying nothing. Then, abruptly, he suggested that they wait in the coffee shop downstairs. "I'll stop at the desk and let them know where to find us."

Still dazed by the sudden horror that had descended upon the safari, Laurie sat opposite Ron a few minutes later, sipping gratefully at her black coffee. There seemed to be nothing to say — nothing and everything.

Ron expressed her thoughts. "Waiting is the most agonizing thing you can do in a hospital. Nothing you can do to help."

Laurie stared into her cup. "I know. I didn't really start shaking until the staff here took over. While there was something we could do. . . ."

"It was different, wasn't it? Back there, I wasn't seeing one of my best friends, or. . . ." Ron hesitated, probably wondering how to designate Eddy without sounding either harsh or hypocritical. ". . . or a kid that risked his life to save Toshi. They were patients. I knew what to do, you knew what to do. I felt like everyone else there was insignificant. There were just . . . the patients and the nurse and. . . ."

"The doctor?" Laurie asked.

Ron's typical nonchalance was lost in an embarrassed blush. "Sure. *Doctor.*" It was a contemptuous dismissal, but there was a wistful quality in his voice, too. "Anyone who's taken a first-aid course could have done what I did. You could have handled it alone."

"Both of them?" Laurie shook her head. "No. Ron, don't you remember? You took charge. It came to you so naturally. I was looking to you for instructions."

Ron looked over at her, his blue eyes questioning. "You were?"

"I was thinking strictly in emergency room terms; stop the bleeding, prevent shock. You —" Laurie shuddered, remembering the scene, "— you were thinking ahead, to a technique that goes far beyond minimum emergency care. At the time, I almost resented the time you were taking to pack Toshi's arm in ice."

"It may still be a mistake," Ron said. "One of those calculated risks — delaying the hospital trip, on a longshot chance that we'd get to a surgeon who knows reimplantation techniques. Or believes in them. A lot of doctors don't think the operation is worth the discomfort."

"I don't understand," Laurie admitted.

"Well, it's new. The first successful reimplantation only dates back to 1962, and of the thirty-odd times it's been attempted since, only about ten operations can really be called complete successes. By that I mean, cases where the patient regained function of the severed limb after it was replaced by surgery. The operation is still in the experimental stages, and some surgeons feel that artificial limbs are preferable. Prostheses are so highly developed today that an artificial limb that functions is, they feel, better than a natural one that doesn't."

"Dr. Wellman belongs to the new school then," Laurie said. She had only caught a glimpse of the Australian surgeon, but Ron had talked to him briefly, earlier.

Ron drained his coffee cup. "Let's say he decided the attempt was worth the gamble. The odds aren't good, Laurie. As he pointed out just before Tosh' was wheeled into surgery, a lot depends on the condition of the severed limb." Ron closed his eyes for a moment. "It wasn't a clean cut. The miracle is that the arm was almost all

185

there. There'd have to be another miracle in reconstructive surgery. And in Toshi's condition — I don't know."

Laurie checked her watch. "He's still in surgery."

"It's a long operation," Ron said. "Six, seven — maybe eight hours, or more."

They were quiet again, Laurie projecting herself into the familiar atmosphere of the white-tiled room somewhere above them. Was Ron there, too? she wondered. Working, instead of waiting — applying skill and knowledge, instead of wondering?

He must have been sharing Laurie's thoughts, for after a long while, Ron said, "I'd rather be in that O.R. than down here."

"So would I," Laurie told him. "Every time I've watched a patient being wheeled to Recovery after an operation, even though I didn't do any more than hand instruments to the surgeons, I've — felt *whole*, somehow. I guess you'd call it fulfillment. You're glad you were there. You want to have the feeling over and over again. I'd give anything if I could cancel what happened today, but —" Laurie's eyes had suddenly filled with tears. "Since it happened, Ron — I'm glad we were there."

"Over and over again," Ron was mumbling to himself. "You save a life, and you come alive yourself. And it's not a once-in-a-lifetime thing. You do it every day. Sometimes, three, four, five times a day."

"In surgery, yes."

A distant, removed expression had clouded Ron's eyes, as though he were looking beyond Laurie, far beyond this place and this time. Then, abruptly, he started talking about Toshi, about how much surfing meant to him, of how being crippled and never being able to challenge the ocean again would be worse for him than dying, because there was nothing more agonizing than a death in life. "It's something like surgery," Ron said. "You're out there, all alone, a peak forms, and it's only you, putting your knowledge and your skill against a tremendous force of nature. Sometimes you lose, but when you come screaming down a twenty-foot smoker, for a few minutes the whole world belongs to you." Ron paused. "I don't suppose I've made my point. It's a — crazy analogy. But, for me, it's valid. Anyway, I know why it's Toshi's whole life."

"I'm sorry I didn't try it," Laurie said. "Maybe I'd understand you if I had."

Ron reached across the table to touch

her hand lightly. "This is hardly the time to try to get you interested," he said. "But in the Islands, at some of the easy beaches, why didn't you let me teach you?"

"You never offered to," Laurie said. She looked at her watch again, without really noticing the time. "Maybe I'll try it alone someday. On my days off. When I get back to California."

She didn't tell Ron how soon she would be going home. Somehow, Laurie thought, it was understood.

They were in the reception room again, and midnight had come and gone, when a weary, middle-aged doctor, still wearing his green surgical jacket, approached them.

Ron was on his feet instantly, Laurie following suit.

"The charge nurse said you were still here," Dr. Wellman said. Deep lines creased his forehead, and fatigue dragged at his footsteps. He looked like a man who has exceeded the maximum point of exhaustion and is drawing on some auxiliary source of energy to keep him going. "Your young friend is in the recovery room. He has an amazing physique, exceptional stamina."

"The operation, Doctor?" Ron's expression begged for an affirmative reply.

"Let's see," the doctor recalled, "you were the young man I talked to earlier — you'd evidently read some article on reimplantations? Yes. We're always grateful when someone outside the profession shows such keen judgment."

Dr. Wellman was justifiably tired; he had been in surgery for more than six hours. But this exasperating slowness! He was drunk with tiredness, droning like someone on the edge of sleep. "Please . . ." Laurie whispered.

"Of course, it's too early for a sound prognosis," the doctor said. "All I can tell you is that young Nomura is holding up remarkably well. As to the reimplantation —" Dr. Wellman seemed to be searching, now, for words that laymen would comprehend. "It will be a long time before we can assess the results. Cosmetically, functionally, in terms of touch and pain sensations — we simply must wait. However, a short time ago, my assistant removed a clamp from — I don't want to confuse you with technical jargon — a clamp from an artery." He demonstrated by pinching his upper arm between his thumb and forefinger, then releasing the grip. "Visualize something like this."

Laurie, to whom clamps were more familiar than manicure scissors, nodded impatiently. Ron merely waited.

"It was one of those dramatic moments that we don't expect the layman to understand," Dr. Wellman said. "You can't know the electricity that ran through the theater. One moment, our patient's arm was cold — white as wax. In the next, the color was pink. A nurse touched the patient's hand and it was warm. Am I making myself clear? The circulation had been restored. We have every right to hope."

Laurie looked from Doctor Wellman's face to Ron's and then back again. It was impossible to decide which revealed more suppressed eagerness. Then, before anyone could start to ply him with questions, the surgeon squared his shoulders and assumed a professionally conservative pose.

"I don't usually carry on this way," Dr. Wellman said gruffly. "You must realize — it's quite new. We are just beginning to learn. Even small successes at this stage tend to. . . ."

He didn't finish the sentence, letting his words drift off in a mist of weariness. But he had almost been apologizing for his excitement, Laurie thought. As though admitting to a triumphal cry in the operating room would have demeaned him in the eyes of "nonprofessionals!"

"I *am* dreadfully tired," Dr. Wellman said. "I could do with a spot of tea." He took time only to let Ron and Laurie thank him, and to mention that the other patient, "young Barclay," was being given a chance to regain his strength before grafts were taken to repair his damaged limbs. When they had exchanged good nights, Dr. Wellman nodded curtly and turned to shuffle down a long, night-dimmed corridor beyond the charge desk. He walked like any exhausted man in his early fifties. But while Ron and Laurie waited for their elevator, they watched his slow progress, and Ron said, "Don't let that stooped shuffle fool you. He's ten feet tall and he's bouncing."

On the way down to the ground floor, Laurie was the first to speak. "I liked him, but that artery clamp bit was a little patronizing."

"It figures," Ron said. "He didn't know you're a nurse." He was thoughtfully silent after that. Dr. Wellman had been talking down to *him*, too. Probably because he didn't know that Ron had once wanted to be a surgeon.

Fifteen

Several week-old newspapers lay open on the table between the two hospital beds. One of the glaring headlines, of the type to which the Australian press seems addicted, screamed, "YANK SURFER HERO IN SHARK ATTACK!" Several subcaptions in bold print announced, "TWO MAULED BY NINE-FOOT MONSTERS," "TEEN-AGER BRAVES DEATH TO RESCUE FRIEND."

"I told Toshi to throw those papers away," Eddy Barclay said. He looked pale, but considering the ordeal he had survived and the long medical treatment still before him, he sounded amazingly chipper. "They don't say anything about why Toshi was off his board in the first place."

"Bruddah, why you talk da kine?" Toshi asked. He smiled weakly at Ron and Laurie. "I keep telling this knucklehead, it's a rider's responsibility to know what's in front of him." He shifted his position in the bed, wincing slightly at the movement of his bandaged shoulder.

"Hurts," Laurie said sympathetically.

Toshi turned on his Island grin. "Yeah. So does this." He pinched the index finger of his left hand gleefully. "I *feel* it! Pinch it, it *hurts*, man. Crazy!" He turned a sober face toward Ron. "I was telling Linc, like, I'm sorry I blew his safari. You know what he said? Maybe it was a good thing. Maybe ole Tercotte found out what he's good for. That — ice jazz. That was the end, man."

"I read a really interesting little squib in the paper once," Eddy piped. "There was this medical missionary in Guatemala, and he did the same kind of operation on a little girl who . . ."

"*Most* people don't *know* this," Toshi interrupted, rolling his eyes to stare at the ceiling.

Eddy made a wry face. "Anyway, it shows how handy it is to know unusual facts. Like Ron knowing about the ice." He reflected on his words for a moment. "You learned that in school, though, huh, Ron?"

"That's right," Ron said.

"Yeah. Well, I've been thinking. Some of this stuff I keep learning — you can't *use* it. Know what I mean? If you're going to learn

193

things, they ought to do you some good. If you learned a lot of things about one subject, like, say, advertising . . . I like to dream up gimmicks and play around with words . . . you could apply it." He looked to Ron for encouragement. "I was talking to my dad about the stupid ads he runs for the drugstores. How would it be if he got the people's attention with some really interesting fact, sort of like the old 'Believe it or Not' thing? Get people started reading the ad, and then, pow! First thing they know, they're finding out Barclay's have a big sale on cough syrup and stuff."

"There's more to advertising than you think," Ron said. "You'd have to learn —"

"I was *saying!* How about, after they get me fixed up so I can walk again — how about if I went to college?" Eddy threw out his final argument almost belligerently. "If I could surf like you do, Ron, I wouldn't. But *you're* going back to school in February. Why shouldn't I go back next September?"

"I didn't know that," Laurie said.

Toshi closed his eyes. "It's a very interesting fact about Ron," he said. "Most people don't know it yet."

They said good-bye soon after that, and left the room so that Linc and Eddy's parents could share the visiting hour. Craig and Vivian Barclay were waiting in the corridor outside the room.

There wasn't much to say to the Barclays, or to hear from them. During the past week, Laurie had found herself their confidante again, except that now they poured out their confidences not separately, but in unison. How long it had taken them to realize that Eddy would have to find his own way in the world! Now that near-tragedy had brought the Barclays closer together, and they were bound by fear and aching consciences, how clear it had become; Eddy's love for people had made him a worshipful bore, but it was his strength, too. It was the source of a phenomenal courage. Perhaps, too, with the discovery of his own strength, he would learn to respect himself more. Others would follow his lead.

"It's like a bad dream," Vivian had said at the hotel last night. "We were driving him, demanding that he make us proud of him. We had it all wrong, Laurie. We should have been making him proud of us."

They were trying. They had a long way to go, Laurie thought. But the most anyone can do is try.

Linc commented on that fact as he drove Ron and Laurie to the airport the next morning. "Craig hasn't said one word about being afraid of a suit from Toshi's family. He's just paying the hospital bills and promising that Tosh'll have a job anytime he wants one."

"I can see Toshi working in a drugstore," Ron laughed. "That'll be the day!"

"Not if I can get him back on a surfboard," Linc promised. "And I will. I'll get you back, too, you fink."

"Between operations," Ron said. "You're darn right you will."

Linc turned from the wheel to address Laurie, who sat wedged between the driver and Ron. "I hear he's going to make a surfer out of you, nursie. Between operations, that is. I think you called it 'putting a great sport into its proper perspective,' right, Ron?" Linc didn't wait for an answer. "Great. Only, do me a favor, Laurie. Paddle prone. I can't stand girls with surf knots on their knees. That's one thing I've always admired about Diane. She has beautiful legs."

"The Princess of Cool," Ron said. (Earlier, he had made a long speech about how much he detested people who lost their heads at the sight of blood.) "She didn't even stop to find out if Tosh' and Eddy survived. She headed back home without even saying 'later.' "

"Do you blame her?" Linc asked face- tiously. "I mean, how friendly can you stay after your boyfriend instructs another dame to knock you cold with a haymaker?"

"You had your back turned," Laurie reminded him. "You didn't see me hit her."

"I *heard* it," Linc said. "And to my trained ear, it sounded like — assuming the circumstances had been a little less de- pressing — a soulfully *satisfying* hay- maker."

He was shaking Ron's hand at the air- port a while later, and leaning down to plant a noisy kiss on Laurie's forehead. The safari was over, but Linc would go on. With or without a Craig Barclay to back him, Linc would go on to Peru. Films would accumulate in South Africa. He wasn't finished with the land "down under" yet. And there was always Sunset Beach, there was always the Pipeline. Laurie could visualize him on a day when he could no longer ride the waves, rolling his wheelchair to the sands before Makaha and Waimea, Haleiwa and Portlock, setting up his tripod, the music of insistent guitars racing through his head, carrying on his endless affair with his only love. As he waved to Ron and Laurie (Linc's cool, casual wave), even the color of his eyes reflected the image of his mistress in one of her stormy moods. Only the sea, Laurie thought, could look more gray. And more lonely. And more free.

"Linc's a graceful loser," Ron said as the jet circled over the sprawling city with its lacy white edging of wave-lashed bays. "How many guys do you meet — dedicated bachelors who get hung up on a girl, propose to her, get accepted, and then still act that civilized when another guy moves in on them?"

He may as well have been talking to Laurie in Swahili. "Are you talking about *Linc?*"

"About Linc," Ron said. "About you. About me."

"*Linc* told you . . ."

"That he was going to settle down and get married. Sure. Well, it's *true*, isn't it? He fixed it up so that you'd come along on the safari after he'd dated you a few times, and you wanted to be together, so . . ."

Laurie wasn't certain herself whether she was laughing or crying. "You didn't *believe* him?"

"Why would I have been knocking myself out trying to make you jealous if I didn't believe him? He *couldn't* have been putting me on! One time, on the beach, I saw the two of you together and I —" Ron had turned in his seat to grasp Laurie's shoulders. "Laurie, you weren't playing games with me? After we broke up, I was mad as sin with you, but I was madder at myself. Then, just about the time I was going to call you, Linc told me . . . he said . . ."

Ron was exploring her eyes for an explanation, and Laurie moved closer to him as she said, "Linc's a great talent, Ron. If I wasn't so fond of him, I'd say he was the most clever liar in the world."

She was in his arms, swift as lightning, smothered, unaware of other passengers, other times. "He nearly overdid it," Ron was murmuring against her ear. "I almost had myself convinced that it didn't matter, I didn't care, I didn't love you." Ron waited until he had pressed his lips against Laurie's and found the response he wanted. "I didn't know it half enough until I saw you out there with those god-awful fins cutting the water. And you swimming the wrong way, like that kooky kid! Swimming right *for* them! Laurie — oh, man, Laurie, if I didn't know it before, I knew it then!"

Laurie kissed *him*, this time. "I have something to tell you, too, Ron." She let him hold her, missing the sight of the exciting city below them, a city that boasted superb waves and a brilliant surgeon — Ron's next two loves after herself. "It's a very interesting fact," she said. Their lips met again. And it would have been incorrect, with so many eyes glued in their direction, to add, "It's something most people don't know."